The Westwood Witches

A Secret Discovered

By

Sarah Northwood

For Abi and Bronwyn, life with you is magical!

I'd like to add a special mention to my daughter Bronwyn, who not only helped me sort out those troublesome sentences but kept my spirits up and encouraged me to keep going. I love you both more than you know!

To my beta readers, Brian and Helen, your feedback was wonderful, thank you. A special thank you, Brian, for yet another wonderful cover.

To Helen, I don't know what I'd do without you. I hope you know how special you are.

To my ever patient and loving husband, where would I be without you?

For you my dearest readers, if you enjoy this story, I'd be so grateful if you could help me by posting a review on Amazon and or Goodreads.

Contents

Prologue

Aero had always been fascinated by Grandma Joanna's ability to turn up at family events just at the right time. It appeared to her that Grandma had a special sense when things were about to turn ugly. Then suddenly she would arrive, with a few new magic tricks up her sleeve, to be greeted with a chorus of oohs and ahhs.

Whatever argument had been about to break out would disappear and every family member from the youngest who could just about sit up, to the eldest who needed a comfy chair to sit down on, would gather around and pay attention. Joanna would give her signature cough, announcing to all that the show would begin, and a hush fell over the room. Every single person waited with anticipation to see what new magic she came up with.

Aero loved everything about her grandma, even the way her grey thinning hair flopped about as she leant forward to give one lucky person the chance to choose a card. She always tipped her own chair and herself as far forward as possible, hoping she might get picked. Sometimes she was!

Aero relished the way her grandma's tired eyes were still playful. They would sparkle with something that looked almost like the sun had slipped inside them, as the excitement in the magic trick mounted.

The ability to diffuse a situation with a few card tricks might not seem incredible but Grandma Joanna's tricks were mesmerising. You could say that her granddaughter wanted nothing more in life than to be exactly like her.

Aero's family was close, even those who she thought of as aunts and uncles but were distant relatives. Her dad was an only child and her mum had one sister; with all the joys a family brings, disagreements seemed to be a natural part of the equation.

Family gatherings were something of a regular event in the family home, usually marking the beginning of a school holiday or a weekend, and were almost always held at the Westwoods' house.

Inevitably, at some point a discussion between a couple or sometimes more of the guests would turn darker and an argument would erupt. They loved to speak out on all kinds of things, and though it took a while before Aero understood what they were arguing about, she couldn't help but be entertained by the sheer theatre of it all.

It was then that Grandma would appear, as if summoned on command, and lo and behold the rows would be forgotten. The partying could continue, often into the late hours of the night. Life was magical.

Grandma Joanna, grey-haired, with a tall thin face, which looked like worn-out leather, had been that way for as long as Aero could remember. She simply never seemed to age, and all was well with the Westwoods, her family, until that dark day Grandma passed away.

As she was elderly, Aero supposed she should have expected it, but death has a way of creeping out from dark corners and taking you by surprise. To this day, she wasn't sure exactly how old Grandma had been when she died, but whatever the age it was too young, as far as she was concerned.

She remembered it well, because not only did Aero lose her great love and hero but the year marked her seventeenth birthday, and although she didn't know it then, everything would change.

It was this year the secrets of the Westwood family were exposed, when Aero learned Grandma Joanna had been murdered. A year when something dear was lost and more than one thing was discovered.

Chapter One

*F*or a few seconds Acro imagined herself still warm and cosy in bed, the covers wrapped around her, peaceful and serene. With a groan, she reluctantly went downstairs. Her mother was sat on the armchair in her usual comfy spot, positioned perfectly in the room to give her a suitable vantage point where she could see the tea coming from the kitchen. Whilst Aero could hear the clink of cups coming from the room beyond, the conversation between her grandmother and her dad was muffled.

She stretched out the kinks of sleep and said good morning to her mum, who only vaguely acknowledged her presence, too engrossed in her planning for the day to offer more. Her mood seemed unusually sour, given the evening's upcoming event. Aero grumbled to herself about the cold, before settling onto the sofa. Shivering, she wrapped a blanket around her shoulders.

More muffled sounds came from the kitchen. Whilst she still couldn't make out the conversation, she recognised Grandma's distinctive voice. Aero smiled. She loved her grandma. Still, she was surprised to see her here so early. She generally disapproved of all the fuss required in the preparation for a party, choosing instead to arrive late, with a dramatic entrance. She fished around for the last time they had all been in the house together this early in the day, but it wouldn't come.

"Are you hungry, love?" Dad's voice boomed from the kitchen. Evidently, he must have heard she was up, despite being in the kitchen. In response, Aero heard her stomach growl. Whilst she was ready for breakfast, her stomach was anticipating what was to come later in the day. Parties at The Westwood house were legendary, and not just for the food.

"Some toast would be great, thanks," she replied.

It was nice having her dad around for a change. He was always heading off to some other part of the country, sometimes abroad. His schedule unpredictable, he went when and where work could be found. It often left her feeling like her life was a merry-go-round and, at some point, she would get thrown from an innocent-looking carousel horse.

Later that evening, Aero helped her mum lay out the posh crockery and tablecloth, ready for the guests. It seemed something of an extravagance for the party food that would grace its surface, but Aero did as her mum told her. Aero's mum had also gently suggested her father take a walk before the guests arrived. She thought her mother found it strange having him underfoot, often wafting him away with a dishcloth or whatever else was to hand. Whilst her mum would never openly admit to it, she'd got used to doing things her own way and being in charge.

"So how was school today, Aero? Did you hang out with Millie?" Mum asked.

"Oh, it was good, thank you, and no, not really."

"I thought you two were friends now?" she enquired.

Aero slipped a sausage roll off the table and stuffed it in her mouth, hoping that would prevent any further interrogation. Her mum was always trying to find ways to help her make new friends. Millie and she had worked together for a few weeks on an art project, but a few classes together did not make them friends as far as either were concerned. Millie had suffered the annoyance of having to work with her and Aero had done her best to keep her mouth closed and her ideas to herself.

"No, she's friends with Andrew's group and Harriet."

"Oh, that's too bad. She seemed nice."

Aero shrugged her shoulders and mumbled with her mouth still full, "We don't really see each other to be honest, Mum."

"Well, at least you've still got Lilly," her mum replied wistfully.

Aero wiped the crumbs from her mouth to cover her trembling lips. She always felt like such a disappointment.

As if by magic, just then her grandma reappeared in the kitchen. Aero had no idea when she'd slunk off but was grateful for her return to ease the tensions. Her grandma looked kindly at them both, but beneath her wiry eyebrows her auburn eyes sparkled with rebellion. Wearing her bright pink top and soft chino trousers, she looked nothing like an 'old person.' Aero found herself staring for a moment, trying to decipher how she managed to pull off a look meant for someone much younger.

"Well then, what have we got here?" Grandma enquired. "You've not been getting into trouble again, have you, my darling girl?" she added playfully.

"No, I haven't, honestly Grandma, I've been as good as gold." Aero shrugged her shoulders and put out her hands, as if to say, what're you going to do?

"Oh, who needs gold? The world needs more of you." Grandma reached out and tapped her nose. "Perhaps that's enough of that kind of talk. After all, we've got a party to look forward to."

Aero's mum sniffed the air. "The pizza's burning, apparently." She turned on her heels and sprinted swiftly to the oven. Then, as if remembering the list of jobs held only in her head, asked, "Mum, can you be a love and carry on helping Aero set up the table?"

Grandma gave a bright smile. One which Aero caught and kept for herself. Aero did her best to carry on with the table setting as Grandma did her best to play along with her daughter's wishes. She gave a little rub of her back, her body slouched, and suddenly Grandma looked as if every year were hanging off her shoulders. She hunkered over and complained bitterly about her aching back. Aero's mum glanced over from the kitchen, her knowing look saying she'd seen this trick before, but her face softened as she took pity. "Well..." she started to say, but then her phone bleeped with a text message, distracting her from her train of thought. Grandma winked mischievously at Aero.

Meanwhile, Dad had returned from his walk and settled down in the living room. All three of them, even Mum, raised an eyebrow when they heard the clink of the rum bottle being opened. Dad tended to enjoy these events a little too much on the odd occasion! Still, he deserved to relax.

As the doorbell rang, Mum's face lapsed into horror. The guests were beginning to arrive. Her tempo in the kitchen increased and with a subtle nod, she gave Grandma and Aero permission to leave.

As the guests began to file in, Dad ensured everyone had a drink and some nibbles in hand. Soon, the low hubbub of conversation became a throb as more and more people gathered in the living room. Mum had collected as many spare chairs as she could muster earlier that day, but still, a good few took to sprawling on the rug, or milling about in the kitchen or conservatory. There was a hint of anticipation in the air.

As much as Aero enjoyed these events, she wasn't much for mingling and took herself to the only quiet spot in the house, the hall. She smiled when she saw her grandma had gone there too.

"Do you think I'll ever be able to get a decent picture of myself up on the wall?" Aero asked with a sigh.

"Oh, give over, you look beautiful. Although these days I almost don't recognise you, you've grown so much," Grandma replied with a hint of pride in her voice.

Aero considered that to be a good thing and decided to ignore the pictures. Her grandma had thought she was beautiful from the moment she had whizzed her way into the world, but Aero was still hoping for a transformation from ugly duckling to swan. She wished it would hurry up, as time was running out. Everyone around her seemed to have made it already but Grandma always told her she would be a late bloomer. Aero frowned. Why did she have to be the last one?

"It's good of your mum to get some pictures up at all. With everything going on, it's a wonder she has time to."

"What do you mean, Grandma?"

"Oh, just with your dad always away these days. She has a lot on her plate, hun." She casually flicked away her hair, which had fallen over her eyes.

"I know, Grandma. Honestly, I do try to make her life easier, it just never seems to work out that way." Aero hunched her shoulders and looked down at the floor.

Her grandma leant forward, her face unusually dark and serious.

"You know something, Aero, you and your mum are a lot more alike than you think. It took her a while to realise how amazing she is too. You'll get there. But listen, love, talking of having a lot on your plate, I just want you to know that I'm going to be a bit busy myself over the next few weeks. So, if I don't see you, just know I've not forgotten you. I could never do that!"

Just then a small commotion broke out in the living room, swiftly followed by Aero's mum popping her head around the door.

"Well, I think it's high time we got this magic show started before there's a war," she said to Grandma.

"Give me a hug for luck then, Aero, my love."

Aero hugged her grandma fiercely and she once again heard the clink of cups as Dad signalled that the show was about to begin. Aero couldn't help thinking that rather than changing, perhaps she'd stay like this forever, if it meant her grandma could too.

Chapter Two

*I*f Pool House Secondary School ever decided to hand out awards for the greatest dork in school, then Andrew Cole, in her humble opinion, would be the undisputed winner. Not only did Aero have to put up with him being in her form group, she had to endure all the other girls in the class fawning over him every day as well. As if he were an adorable puppy, rather than just a boy. It wouldn't annoy her quite so much if he had just been an idiot. The thing that tipped the balance way over into dork land? The fact that he was a good-looking idiot and so incredibly aware of it.

For Aero, this added up to too much to bear. Perhaps she'd care a little less if she'd not been the sole target of his bullying, but for some unknown reason she was. So, as far as she was concerned, Andrew would remain firmly in the land of dorkish territory forever, even without an award. Everyone being under his spell made the whole thing even more unbearably difficult. That is, everyone except her friend Lillith, the one person in Aero's world who made life tolerable at all.

The two were alike, Aero thought. Except Lilly, as Aero fondly called her, was a significantly improved and less troublesome model than herself. Aero felt as far from perfect as any person ever did. Despite having discovered several times over that trouble was a bad thing, and certainly not seeking it out, it always seemed to find her. She likened it to her uncanny ability to be the one stung by the last wasp of the season. Bad luck just had a way of biting her on the butt. Lillith, with all her awesomeness, usually saved her hide and bailed her out of whatever trouble had found her on that particular day. But that wasn't all Aero thought she was good for, far from it. It would be fair to say Aero loved her, as only a best friend could.

Lillith was pretty but seemed yet to properly wear it, as if it were a dress size she still needed to grow into. Taller than her peers, slim with shoulder-length hair, her milk bottle glasses hid round kind eyes beneath them, causing her to often be overlooked because of them. In contrast, Aero's figure was well built, with a face just a touch too round for her liking. Comparing herself with others became a part of Aero's routine and she often found herself falling short. In her own opinion, her worst feature was undoubtedly her hair. Unruly, auburn, sometimes coppery in the sunlight, it refused under any circumstances to be tamed. Aero had spent the last few months growing it longer, hoping the length would balance out her face. Instead, it simply sat on her head like a tangled old skipping rope.

The topic of her hair fuelled Andrew Cole with the most ammunition, although Aero believed she didn't earn herself any favours by being totally immune to his good looks and charm either. Unfortunately, she found herself agreeing with Andrew on one of these things. Her hair did look as if it would make a perfect home for a family of birds. As for the other, she hoped earnestly to never be cured of the ability to see through people. Especially those as shallow as him.

As Aero looked at the purple package of goodies that had been delivered yesterday, she decided it only slightly made up for her grandmother not actually being at her birthday. She couldn't recall her ever missing one before and somehow it had felt like the event wasn't real without her. None of this ever got mentioned to Aero's mum because then she really would seem like nothing more than a foolish girl. Perhaps she'd reached the age where she shouldn't care about things like grandmothers, but she couldn't help the way she felt.

Whilst Aero adored the straighteners, the frizz control hair products, the rose-gold bracelet and make-up her grandmother had sent, she would have much preferred to have seen her instead. Although she had to admit to being impressed with the fabulousness of the gifts. *How did an old woman like her know exactly what she'd wanted?* Still, she wasn't one to look a gift horse in the mouth and she was a sucker for a present.

Perching on the edge of the bed, straighteners in hand, she got ready for the day. With every stroke of the hot steam, the frizz from her hair disappeared, so much so that Aero couldn't resist running her fingers through her silky locks and admiring the sparkle. *Grandma had done good.*

"Aero?" Mum called up the stairs.

Aero paused for a moment before replying. She could already detect a tense undercurrent in her mother's voice. "Yeah?" She swallowed hard, suppressing the urge to sound annoyed by taking a deep breath.

"Come on, hun, you're going to be late." Whilst her mother's voice had a softness to it, she could hear the hint of irritation in the undertone, the suspicion that her daughter had let her down and would be late again creeping into her voice.

"Okay, Mum, I'm coming," Aero shouted back sweetly. She often found herself wondering how on earth her parents could have decided to saddle her with a name like Aeronwen. There were so many perfectly good names out there in the world, which didn't involve the need of a dictionary to spell them. With a bit of persuasion, she'd managed to negotiate the nickname Aero. Thankfully, like her parents, it had stuck around.

When it came to names, what else should she have expected though from a person named Peregrine? Peregrine was her mum's name, but everyone called her Perri for short. She supposed they both had names they wanted to change. Then there was her dad, Xander. This was the kind of stuff you couldn't make up if you wanted to. Thank goodness for Grandma Joanna. At least one of them had a relatively normal name, otherwise Aero would have thought it a conspiracy.

Aero thought that her mum's voice had reached that slightly awkward phase between soft and screechy. Aero could imagine her skulking around in the living room, looking up at the clock on the mantlepiece and beginning to panic. Her mum, whilst a practical kind of person, tended to think Aero incapable of doing anything right, let alone making the bus on time. Aero knew that in many ways her mum was right, but perhaps if she would let her at least try, she might have a chance to prove her wrong.

Still, she couldn't blame her really. She had missed the bus on more than one occasion. If there were anyone keeping a list of faults, she thought them wise to go ahead and add tardiness to hers.

"Hunny, are you nearly ready? You don't want to miss the bus again!"

"Just coming, Mum." She put the straighteners down on her dressing table, wincing slightly as she caught her fingers on the edge of them. *Those things are hot!* She switched them off at the plug; the last thing she wanted to do was burn the house down on her first day of using them. With one last look in the mirror, satisfied, Aero snatched up her rucksack. Taking the stairs at a sprint, she tripped, but she reached out and managed to grab hold of the bannister to save herself from a broken leg. *Ah, it's going to be one of those days*, she thought.

Her mum smiled warmly. "Have a great day, hun. Love you."

"Love you too," Aero replied.

Perri listened to the soft shush of the door closing behind her and felt a long breath release from her body, relieved her daughter hadn't fallen and broken her leg. Mornings were such a stressful affair. She meandered towards the kitchen, in search of a healing cup of tea.

Aero would always be her baby. It was true what they said about a mother's love for a child; no one could prepare you for the intensity, the joy, the worry, but there were moments like these when she wished her daughter had things together just a little bit more. Especially when she knew the burden that Aero may yet have to face.

Chapter Three

Thankfully Aero didn't have to go too far to catch the bus, which she thought of as a blessing, not only because of her lateness but because her legs were the kind not built for running. One left turn out of Cauldon Avenue, and then another left onto Heath End Road. About halfway up on the other side of the road, underneath the street light, the bus collected her and all the other children, having first driven around the other side of the estate to pick up the kids there, before doubling back along the roads of the estate to collect them. This meant they didn't have to walk further up and wait on the busier high street.

Clutching a small but perfectly functional blue lunch bag, which swung back and forth at her side with every bouncing step, Aero felt lively for a change, despite the rough start to the morning. Tugging her coat tightly around her, she tried to ward off the early morning chill. As usual, a beaming smile greeted her as Aero caught sight of Lillith up ahead, already at the stop.

Smiling back at her was a reflex action, as natural as breathing. There was nothing better than seeing her friend to make her feel good about the day ahead. Aero picked up the pace, grinning back, and for the first time since waking up that morning felt like everything was going to be okay. Moving closer, Aero could see Lilly dancing on the spot to keep warm.

"Hi, Aero. Wow, I love your hair," Lilly said.

She felt the heat rise to her cheeks in reply as Lilly reached out to touch her friend's new hairdo in amazement. "Thanks. How are you feeling today? Are you doing okay after last night?"

Nodding, Lilly replied, "Are you kidding me? It was a fantastic party. I'm feeling on top of the world. Thanks for inviting me."

"You know full well it wouldn't have been the same without you. You're the only one I liked there. Come to think of it, you're the only one I actually knew," Aero replied.

"What about Fred?" Lilly asked.

"What about Fred?" Aero replied, giggling.

Lilly blew her a kiss just as the bus pulled up to the kerb. They'd taken the same bus together since Aero started at Pool House Secondary School, which they'd attended for a couple of years now. It hadn't been long before they'd become firm friends. Something new. Something Aero still struggled to believe could be true. Her luck, she mused, was generally not that good.

It came as no surprise then, that the two had ended up staying on together in the sixth form college, lovingly known as Pool House. Which essentially took place in the top two floors of the Parker building of their school, and was nowhere near as glamourous as it sounded. The only significant difference, but by far the most important, was that they no longer had to endure the starchiness and horrid burgundy of the school blazer.

Making friends had been an issue for Aero for as long as she could remember. Not because she hadn't wanted to blend in at the other schools she'd attended before. She'd wanted nothing more than to have friends and be like everyone else. Before Lilly though, she'd always stuck out like a sore thumb. Wanting to fit in but knowing she would always be an outsider, as if everyone else were aware of some secret that she did not know. At times it felt like there was some great conspiracy taking place. In truth, she'd always felt out of sync with life, different, but with Lilly they found themselves out of sync together. She didn't have to feel lonely or afraid anymore.

Making connections with people had been difficult for Aero since she'd learned it was something others did naturally. Her lifestyle probably hadn't helped. They had to move to a new house and town often for her dad's work, which made putting down roots not only impossible but also a waste of time. *Why make the effort to grow friendships which will be uprooted before they can bloom?*

Which came first, difficulty with trusting people, or every time she got close to someone they'd move on to a new house again, Aero didn't know. The one constant and friend through it all remained her grandma, Joanna. Joanna had always found a way to make it to

Aero's birthday before. Wherever they were, she would be there. She supposed having a grandma as a best friend wasn't a bad thing really. She had a treasure chest of fond memories to dive into when things were difficult, but it wasn't the same as having a friend her own age. Which made meeting Lillith so incredible and important to her. For all kinds of reasons, she made the effort worthwhile.

The pattern of starting at a new school had always been the same for Aero. She would be asked to stand at the front of the class for an introduction. A hush would come over everyone as they assessed the vulnerabilities of the newbie. As she headed to the back of the classroom (it was always the back), one by one, she would weave her way through the desks, the other kids shuddering and turning away, as if she had a disease or something.

But Lilly... she'd looked right up at her and said hello. Her thick glasses were tilted up at her, but all Aero could see was the warmth of her smile. If home is where the people you love are, then 42 Cauldon Avenue in the village of Scholarly Wood felt like the first home Aero had ever truly had. It seemed to her that even her mum and dad had grown fond of the place; after all they had settled here, against their natural instincts.

Aero looked over at her friend and saw that she didn't want to face the scrum of kids jostling to get on the bus any more than she did. So they both waited for the rush to die down before attempting it.

"Don't you think they ought to at least put on a double decker or another bus or something?" Aero asked, scanning the crammed seats for two spots together.

All the younger kids who'd started back in September still had a wide-eyed look of fear etched upon their faces. Aero smiled at them as they made their way through, and thought to herself, *At least for the time being, I'm over the horror of being new here.*

As they walked passed Andrew Cole, Aero made a point of putting her nose in the air. Though secretly, she hoped he would notice her. Or rather, notice her hair. Neither girl waited around to find out. *There.* Pointing at last to two seats together, they found their way over, wobbling from side to side as the bus had already started up again.

"All right?" Fred from Aero's tutor group asked. He was sat in front of them. Aero glanced up quickly, smiled and nodded as they settled in to their seats, Lilly by the window and Aero in the aisle. They did their best not to breathe through their noses. The bus always smelt like week-old washing, but they almost didn't notice it anymore. Aero thought that given enough time you could become acclimatised to any bad stuff until it seemed practically normal.

"So how does it feel to be seventeen?" Lilly said.

"Yeah, it's so completely different," Aero answered sarcastically, neither quite containing their giggles. *Thank God Lilly gets my wacky sense of humour, because frankly no one else on the planet does*, she thought.

"Fancy going to see a movie this weekend?" Lilly asked.

"Yeah, all right, if we don't have to do that design project. You know what Mr Brian is like for springing things on me last minute. What about you, you won't have a date?"

"Nah. With these things?" Lilly wiggled her glasses up and down to emphasise her point.

Under her breath, she whispered, "But, maybe we could invite Fred, if you like?"

Saturday would be Valentine's Day but Aero couldn't imagine spending the day with anyone else. Snorting, Aero choked back a howl of laughter and smiled. Lilly knew Fred liked her but also knew she had no intention of having a boyfriend. Instead, she opted for those in books that she could pick up and leave whenever she chose.

The bus swung out of the village and onto the main road, into the town of Essence Pool. Without a pause, both girls switched into school mode, preparing themselves for the day ahead. The school itself sat next to a large pool, which was how it got its name, and school mode equated to the two of them being nerds, but they were more than okay with it. At seventeen, they were all about self-awareness.

Chapter Four

*L*illy and Aero still shared a few classes together, but that morning Aero headed off for technical design with Mrs Wood, and Lilly made her way to English. Lilly was undoubtedly the better writer of the two, but Aero had a talent for art. They often joked that one day they'd write a book together and take over the world. Lilly would bring the stories and Aero would breathe life into them with her pictures. With promises to meet by the lockers out by the drama studio, they arranged to meet up at break time. It had become a familiar routine and one they both looked forward to.

Today's project for Aero was to continue working on a 3D bridge model. Mrs Wood, flashing her kind blue eyes, glanced up momentarily from her desk as Aero entered. The classroom filled up fast as the students ambled to their seats. The challenge Mrs Wood had set with the bridge model was to make it entirely out of recycled materials. Feeling a buzz of enthusiasm rush through her, Aero was eager to begin. The combination of art and engineering brought her sheer joy. It was one of the few lessons she had where writing wasn't a necessity. *Totally a win!*

Andrew Cole was unfortunately sat at the far end of her table, and with Mara and Aaron on either side of him, the endless drone of mindless chatter disturbed her concentration. She craned her head to listen to their conversation. The temptation was too great, even though she knew they were probably talking about her. Aside from the odd burst of chuckling and glances her way, which only made her feel more strongly that she was the topic of their amusing conversation, she'd no idea what they were talking about. Her face flushed with a rosy glow as Andrew caught her listening. She quickly averted her eyes but it was too late, she knew he'd caught her in the act.

His eyes seem to flick over her, his unspoken question asking why she was staring at him. Subconsciously twirling a strand of her hair, Aero looked away again. *He still hadn't noticed.* Ignoring him and turning her attention back to the work in front of her, slowly the world around became hushed. Mrs Wood glanced up from her desk. Her expressive blue eyes had an uncanny ability to make you feel like she saw everyone in the room at once, but Aero didn't notice her at all. Instead, her fingers had taken over the work, moulding, shaping and moving the pieces, one at a time. Engrossed, she didn't even notice as Mrs Wood strolled up behind her chair to look at her progress.

The jingle of the classroom door made her jump out of her skin and almost drop the hot glue gun she'd been using. *Darn it.* Aero and the rest of the class couldn't help but look up at this intrusion when the door opened. For Aero's classmates, pure curiosity drove their wide-eyed stares, but for Aero, her eyes demanded to know who had messed up her hard work. Her anger washed away quickly, to be replaced with fear. Shivering, her legs began to tremble a little as she saw who had entered. Mr Brian, with Lilly at his side. *Something was wrong. Why was Lilly here?*

∞   ∞   ∞

Mrs Wood had always been rather fond of Mr Brian, he had a kind face and shared her attitude to teaching. Perhaps because they were similar ages, they both had energy and enthusiasm in spades. She saw him look first at her desk and then around the room, until his eyes found hers. Mrs Wood felt disappointed to see his face had no smile today and his eyes held worry in them like lines on a paper. She flashed him a sympathetic smile. It struck her as odd to see that he was accompanied by another pupil, Lillith Jones, which was unusual and alarmed her somewhat. She was aware that Lilly and Aero were friends, having frequently seen them walking the playground together or in the cafeteria. She held her breath, waiting to discover the reason for his visit.

"Apologies for interrupting, Mrs Wood. Please may I borrow Aero Westwood?"

"Of course," she replied softly, making a mental note to check in on her pupil the next time she saw her. Still behind Aero's chair, she gave her a gentle and encouraging pat on the shoulder. A gesture oozing with sympathy. Realising something was indeed wrong, she dismissed Aero swiftly from the class. Behind her a hum of noise had risen in the classroom, the whispering pupils eager to discuss this new and juicy gossip.

"Okay everyone, settle down, back to your projects, please," Mrs Wood said.

Andrew frowned as Aero got up from her seat. Amongst his friends he was a tough guy and someone not to be trifled with. He had a reputation to uphold, a group that looked up to him and expected him to behave a certain way. They all believed he enjoyed the power and thrill of being in control. He quickly plastered a look of disinterest on his face and smiled knowingly to his groupies, joining in with their fun at Aero's discomfort, as she walked past them to leave the classroom.

But the truth of the matter was that, in that moment, the person Andrew liked most in the world was suffering. If he'd been a better man, a stronger one, he would have told her he loved her. He'd thought about it often, all the time. Her hair, her skin, the way her eyes seemed to say they didn't need anyone. He knew it would never happen, that it could never be. If he were to go out with a girl like her, then everything he'd built would be gone. He was as helpless in love as he was now. There wasn't a thing he could do.

Andrew ignored the fact it made him the same as his father and concentrated instead on the joy of not being defenceless. At school there were plenty of 'sensitive' souls to belittle, demean and bully. Aero included. This caused him difficulties in more ways than one. Usually he ignored the voice inside his head easily, which told him things were going too far. The voice which knew that control was nothing more than an illusion and soon there would be no way back.

As she exited the classroom, Aero frantically wracked her brain for what thing she could have done wrong this time. Only then did she stop to ask herself why Mr Brian would bring

Lilly with him, if she were in trouble. There could be no other reason, something dreadful had happened. It seemed the only logical explanation. Keeping her eyes fixed on the floor, Aero didn't dare look up at his face. She knew if she saw Mr Brian's expression, it would only confirm her fears and tell her something she could not bear to hear.

"Lilly?" Aero asked, as Mr Brian informed her they were going to the Head's office. Instead of answering, Lilly reached out and gently held her hand. This set off a ricochet of panic, starting first in Aero's legs, which became unstable and knocked together unceremoniously. Leaning up against Aero to steady her, Lilly whispered, "I've got you."

With a nod, the Head dismissed Lilly, and the two entered the office. Aero saw her mum already inside waiting for them and knew her fears were about to be confirmed. She would be the first to admit she'd seen the walls inside before, having visited on more than one occasion. Being in trouble was something which happened to her frequently. Most definitely though, it happened to her, rather than the other way around. Despite hating the scrutiny and attention being in trouble brought, Aero would gladly have taken a telling off, a detention, anything over the feeling she now had in the pit of her stomach.

Hearing the news that her grandmother had died, the familiar off-white, tired walls were a canvas for a different kind of pain. First came the relief that it wasn't her mum or dad and then the sorrow of knowing her grandma had gone. The walls held a sting which would last forever, instead of just one detention. How she wished she could simply fade into them and disappear. A well-known sensation of loneliness washed over her. As Lilly had left, so too had what little courage she had, but softly she dared to ask, "How can she be dead?"

Staring at her feet, her head swam in confusion. Bereft, she still found the strength to tell herself off. *I'm practically an adult now, get it together. I should be taking the news better than this, but if Grandma Joanna is truly gone, truly... dead, nothing will ever be the same again,* she thought.

Breathing deeply, she tried hard to stem the tears falling down her face, but quickly stopped trying, realising the futility of her efforts. By asking that one simple question, she allowed the reality to enter her heart, and by admitting it, made it real. A torrent of emotion exploded from inside her and for a split second, she felt the room begin to physically spin.

"Aero, honey, I've got you." Her mother's voice was like a soft song inside the eye of a storm, soothing, yet distorted and dreamy. Closing her eyes, she followed the sound, grabbing hold of it like an anchor. Her mother wrapped her soft loving arms around her, providing a shield to the outside world and all its horrors inside a tight hug.

Chapter Five

The night before

Joanna checked her backpack supplies again, noting a water bottle and sandwich. Food and drink were some of the more obvious staples needed for her mission. Lurking at the bottom of the bag were some other things that were less obvious. What she had come to think of as *real-world* gadgets. She still had a hard time with these.

One thing she did need and found useful was a torch. The daylight had already begun to turn. Soon it would be twilight, the worst time for spying. It wasn't yet necessary to take any cover from this distance, yet she still felt a sense of urgency and broke into a half walk, half jog.

If, as usual, there had been a choice, Joanna would have cased the house in the daylight. It was probably wrong to assume light offered any kind of mortal protection, but it at least afforded the illusion of one. She wasn't brave, and if it hadn't been for her unique skills, she wouldn't be here at all. Joanna complained to herself as she tracked along the pavement. Grumbling and muttering under her breath, each stride landed with a vicious thud on the pavement beneath her feet. Her temper was made all the worse because she had missed out on her granddaughter's birthday for the first time in her life. But the importance of this mission overrode everything, and she understood she had become a victim of her own past successes.

Together with the British secret service, she'd been a part of operations like this one for about five years, give or take. Much to the dismay of her dear daughter Perri, who despised the thought of her putting herself in danger. Family was family, what choice did she have?

The Westwoods were proud and had always tried to use their power for good, to help those in need. It was an almost forgotten heritage now. Joanna felt a duty to continue the legacy, before there was no one else left to fight. Of course, the fight had changed somewhat. She now worked for the government in exchange for keeping her own family safe, to keep them anonymous.

In the past there were those witches who'd bucked the secret life, but their exposure had put them all in danger. With modern technology, they were more easily tracked, more easily exposed. Secrecy was imperative. Joanna didn't know who else was left out there now and as far as she knew, they were the last of their kind.

At the end of Cranage Grange on the outskirts of the town, far beyond their new home town, she came to a rundown area in need of attention. Up ahead on the right, she approached one of these large abandoned houses. Like most of the buildings along here, it hadn't seen love in a long time. The mortar holding the bricks together was crumbling away, and the once shiny terracotta roof tiles had become aged with moss and weather. Her piercing eyes remained vigilant, however, as appearances could be deceptive. The corner of the street provided her with a good vantage spot, perfect for spying on the covert activity of the target.

A little further along lay tonight's destination, a disused and long since vacant warehouse. The housing estate had originally been built for the workers of a factory which had gone broke and then become re-purposed. Like the factory before it, the warehouse had also failed. Perhaps the place was cursed?

Crossing over to the other side of the road, it was time to take up the offer of increased cover provided by the shadows of some large oak trees. Joanna felt her chest thudding and the tingle of adrenalin pump extra energy into her legs. On the other side of the street, Joanna's team was nearby. Located inside a black van, stripped of any distinguishing features, the team tracked her movements. The earpiece in her left ear began to fill with voices shouting instructions. *Do not engage, reconnaissance only. Survey and secure the information, maintain radio silence.* Team '*Achilles*' was a go.

The warehouse was less than fifty meters ahead. Joanna began to swing around further to the left, keeping under cover. She didn't want her approach to be detected. Hence, why she'd ventured out here alone. It wasn't a meet and greet. Darkness consumed the last of the light and Joanna breathed a little easier. She preferred the blackness which could smuggle away her outline.

The simple aim of this mission was to assess and retrieve information only. Slowing down, treading carefully so as not to fall, her eyes adjusted a little more to the dark. The surrounding grounds were as shadowy as if a blanket had swept over them, the warehouse in front emitting no guiding light. It was soothing to her, but perilous to the untrained eye. It didn't matter, Joanna thrived in the shadows. She was a witch after all. Although she could have used magic to provide a light, or in fact the torch in the rucksack, she chose to remain in the darkness, the world around her now virtually invisible.

She noted that the outer layer of the building at the front had been constructed mostly from metal. Evaluation of what lay behind its façade could not be assessed from there. A single storey high, wider than its height, it had no windows at the front. The entrance was merely a rusted corrugated metal roll door, there was no information to be gained through only observing. Cautious of where she placed her feet, Joanna's footfalls made no sound. Continuing around the side of the building, she scanned for a window or doorway to gain entry, despite her instructions.

This was a no contact operation, but she knew from experience nothing could be gained without a little risk. Perhaps that was the heart of the truth of why she had come. Maybe morals and quests to do good were nothing more than a desire to use magic. To feel the burn of the power underneath her skin.

The modern age had taken away the necessity for most spells. Who needed a spell to cast a curse to hurt someone when a bullet would easily do the same job? Joanna knew it wasn't as simple as that. It was a case of adapt or die. The time for her to get to grips with the interweb thingy, the digital age, had passed, but she knew the future when she saw it. Her granddaughter's face popped into her mind... *perhaps Aero?*

All things had to evolve to move forward, to remain the same was to wither away to nothing. Joanna did not think magic itself should fade. She might be old, but she still believed magic to be a beautiful thing... in the right hands. Her favourite thing in all the world was her cards. When the children's faces lit up at a spell, it brought joy and hope.

Despite understanding magic needed to be kept hidden to ensure their survival, the time had come for the next generation to take up the mantle. Perhaps one day, there would be a world where humans would not fear those who were different.

The potential existed for life to be so much better. No more a world of those who have and those who don't. Or perhaps she thought, she had simply become an old woman who knew all too well how quickly life passed you by. Living a life of deceit and duality proved to be exhausting. Magic or not, eventually everyone headed to the same final destination.

Not everyone in the Westwoods agreed with the view of obscurity being in their best interests. There were those entrenched in tradition who believed magic was the only way. Why use an email when they could simply transmit their thoughts instead? So what if the humans noticed their powers? She remembered, with a sense of irony, those witches who were happy to utilise at least some of the luxuries the modern world had given them. She hadn't met a member of the family without a television and oh, how they loved to watch zombie movies.

Alas, the magic gene was slipping away. Perhaps there would be no place left for it at all soon. Even her own granddaughter had not yet become aware she may in fact be a witch. If indeed, the power had been passed down at all and not skipped another generation, as it seemed prone to do these days. She would not let that happen to Aero.

She had the potential, this child of the digital age. She could teach her new spells. Aero was clever, quirky, brilliant. If she chose to, perhaps she would take up the challenge and bridge the gap between technology and magic. Children, as they say, are the future.

Operation Achilles had been sanctioned directly by the Secretary of Defence, Arianna Campbell herself. Sources had provided intel that this warehouse held the location of an underground group known as the Real Worlders, who were supposedly amassing together the necessary items for a nuclear bomb. It remained unclear who the intended target for the bomb would be, but it was certain it would cause global devastation.

Perri, her beautiful winged daughter, had been right when she'd told her the humans were intent on self-destruction. (Joanna didn't find it strange that she didn't consider herself human.) Often in the name of some religion or other, each truly believed they had sole rights to this world they all thought of as their own.

Their logic, albeit a twisted one, fell short in so far as destruction for the humans most likely meant destruction for the entire world, and that included them. What was known in the government as an extinction level event.

As much as she loved thinking of her family, Joanna urged her brain to be still. She could not sort out all their problems here and now. Turning her attention back to the task, Joanna saw that at the back of the warehouse, the outside of the building was worn away, revealing its structure to be made from bricks and mortar. Joanna also noticed a door but no windows. Talking into the hidden microphone in her jacket, Joanna whispered, '*No viable options for observations, one entry route possible via the back of the building... going in.*'

Throwing her hand to her ear as if it could stop the voices, the ear piece buzzed crazily with demands for her to stop. *'Not sanctioned. Too dangerous. Abort. Dammit, Joanna, don't go in there.'* Ignoring the drone in her ear, she closed her eyes and let the world drift away. Moving unseen between the spaces of the world, she crept closer. Joanna put her hands on the door, and unsurprisingly found it locked. This was where it got exciting.

The stuffiness inside the van began to rise and each breath its occupants took was stale and insufficient. Sweat broke out on Maxwell Chambers' forehead as he realised the risk of losing his potential high value target. As the youngest supervisor of this secret team, there would be hell to pay if the worst should happen. Decisions needed to be made. *Should they move in or let it play out?*

Maxwell looked to his number one guy, a man he trusted to help him make the difficult decisions. The potential for this to go horribly wrong had just jumped up exponentially.

Maxwell felt acutely aware that Arianna would not be happy if that happened. Still, when his man merely shrugged his shoulders, unconcerned, Max breathed a little easier.

Joanna sucked in a deep, cleansing breath, drawing on the power of the Shadow Realm. Placing one trembling hand on the door, she used the other to wipe away the sweat of her exertions from her forehead. Joanna's powers were drawn from the strongest forces in this world. The birth of a new flower, the kindness of a kiss, a baby's smile. Channelled by the creatures who inhabited the realm, the words she uttered were only as important as the meaning beneath them. Knowledge of the right words, their meaning, this higher speech as it was known, gave them power above their own abilities.

It allowed the Westwood witches to draw magic through them, but it required acceptance. Trust for the magic to come through. For Joanna, her source of power drew from the Shadow Realm, but far from being a dark and scary place, she sought the creatures too pure to live in the light. The mystical animals, the long-forgotten ones who had descended into myths and folklore. They existed now together with the Shadow Realm, the creatures' home, from where her power drew forth. She had pledged herself to those creatures, and to only do good.

She held her breath and cast out the spell.

Forces of good now attend, my quest for truth cannot yet end.

Magic power come through me, open this door to set me free.

Joanna felt a heat pass through and out of her. She tried the door again. This time she found it pleasingly unlocked. Before proceeding, she tuned her senses to the noises around her, rather than to the voices in her ear. Hearing nothing, she opened the door. Fumbling through, it was so dark she couldn't even see her hand in front of her face. With zero visibility she relied instead on the sense of sound, but her ears were greeted with only silence. *Perhaps the information they'd received was incorrect?* It wouldn't be the first time.

Back completely in the solidity of the real world, she slipped off the backpack and took out the torch. A small beam of light cut a slice through the blackness. The place had an eerie stillness, even the wittering voices in her ear had gone quiet. As if they too were holding their breaths.

CLUNK! She felt, rather than saw, the lump of wood hit her back. Tilting forward, her body lurched and took a stumbling step. She staggered forward one step and then another to regain her balance. *Ambushed*, she thought.

Still swaying, she got to her feet and swung the torch around in the direction of the attack, only to see the wood coming towards her again. With no choice she ran forwards, swiftly ducking beneath the arc of the wood swinging towards her. She considered using her magic to attack but knew her chances were better if she fled back out into the darkness. Joanna headed out of the door, seeking freedom and escape from her unknown attacker. Breaking radio silence, Joanna spoke in rapid, breathy bursts.

"Ambushed... attacker in pursuit. Target unidentified." Joanna squeezed the words out between gasps of breath as she ran, directionless.

"Do you require assistance?" Supervisor Chambers asked, cursing his decision to allow the night's events to deviate from his well-thought-out plan.

"Negative, team leader. Waste of resources. Mission... Achilles compromised. Making strategic retreat... attempting to escape unseen."

Running hard, Joanna's feet bounced against the uneven ground. Two thoughts occurred to her simultaneously: things were about to get interesting, and she was too old for all this.

Chapter Six

U nder the cloud-covered moonlight, Joanna fled in the opposite direction than the one she'd arrived by. The back of the warehouse led onto woodland, which not only slowed progress but made escape more perilous in the poor light. Joanna wasn't afraid of the shadows. For a witch, they held a mysterious charm, and the joys in life were all about the magical. But shadows, Joanna found, reflected life. It had been her experience that people saw different things within them. Lovers saw places to catch stolen moments, there were those who saw and sought solitude, and of course there were those who saw loneliness. For the first time in her life, Joanna saw death within hers.

She spotted a gap in the trees and quickly made the decision to cut through it to get back to the road and town. If she could get to an open, well-lit place, then she could turn and disarm this unknown person chasing her. Having taken a bloody risk, she didn't want the rest of the team in danger and so held tight to hope and to the slim chance of winning this with no casualties. It was still doable.

A whistling sound whizzed past her ears. At first, she couldn't quite place the source of the noise, until it got closer. *Pop, pop.* Joanna jumped and ducked out of the way. Little shards of earth flew up into the air next to her feet. Realising the source of the noise came from bullets fired in her direction, she needed to be more pro-active. Joanna wasn't invincible, she couldn't simply out-manoeuvre speeding bullets.

Power of shadows, I am your friend, these bullets which fly seek my end.

Cover me now in your finest silk, until my body beneath you sinks.

A familiar feeling of warmth came over her as the magic rushed through her entire body. She brought her hand up to her face, and even though she knew it existed, it seemed to have disappeared. Joanna whispered, "*Invisible.*"

Bang.

Another bullet, this time ricocheting far to the right. Chancing slowing down to catch her breath, Joanna reached the safety of the pavement and found herself back on the edge of the street. She sneaked a look behind her at the pursuer. The man seemed to be looking around and blinking, as if to say, where'd she go?

Yep, that's right, you better believe it. I can disappear.

The boy's face wrinkled up in disapproval. He reached into his camouflaged trousers and fumbled around for something in one of the many pockets. Pulling out some strange-looking goggles, he slipped them over his head. Standing with his feet apart, he scanned the area methodically, searching for something. *Hunting for her.* So far, judging by the anger coming off him in waves, he'd not found her. Not to be deterred, the man began to move in the direction she'd just gone, stopped and tried again. This time he slowly turned a full 360 degrees.

Damn, they must be night vision goggles, Joanna thought. *Or worse, thermal.* Even with the invisibility spell, those things could track her heat signature. With no idea of the range of the glasses, Joanna turned into an alleyway next to the house she'd spotted earlier. Every part of her body ached, the whack the guy had given her was taking its toll. She crouched down, her head hung low. Her legs yelled at her to stop and recover, and so she listened. Waited and hid. It wasn't safe here, but for now she had escaped capture.

Soon she would have to run again. The invisibility spell would last a little longer, but no spell lasted forever. No good spell, anyway. Trapped, for a moment Joanna considered the request for back-up. *No*, she would not willingly put someone else in danger. For magic to work, you had to surrender to its power, you must give in and trust the forces will work for you. Joanna relinquished her fear and surrendered to the will of the realm. If it was destiny to survive, then she would.

Closing her eyes, she felt the slower pulse of her heart beating. For magic to work, you needed a strong heart, and Joanna knew hers had long since begun to fail; an old woman, she had walked the earth for over a hundred years.

A stillness crept over her as she lay huddled in the alleyway. She couldn't risk looking around and had no idea where the man who had been chasing her had gone. With any luck he'd have given up by now.

The shadows parted like an ocean as Joanna saw the huntsman standing over her. Wide-eyed, to her surprise he appeared much younger than she'd thought... far too young to take a life. His fingers twitched nervously on the trigger of the gun. Joanna gritted her teeth and summoned her strength. S*he was not done yet*. Under her breath she whispered a protective spell and rose to her feet. Magic and reality collided as Joanna threw a spell to disarm the boy.

The spell struck its target, but the boy had ducked to the right. He must have anticipated it coming. Bumping against the gravel wall of the alleyway, the boy still held on tight to the gun in his hand. The two danced together, each attempting to get the upper hand. Joanna felt the thud as a bullet bounced off her protective shell. She raised her hands defensively but was shoved backwards by the impact. Just then Joanna smelt the faint tang of metal, and felt a warmth begin to trickle over her chest. Looking down, her eyes grew wide at the sight of an oozing sticky patch of red.

The boy's eye opened wide in horror before he quickly turned and fled.

"Joanna, report. Dammit Joanna, what's happening?" The voice in her ear now screaming, she'd gone past the ability to hear. Destiny had spoken, and the Shadow Realm had come to reclaim one of its own. At last the old woman slept the eternal sleep.

At the sound of gunshots, Maxwell Chambers threw out his earpiece in disgust and the team scrambled out of the van to find out what had happened.

Chapter Seven

ero's home at 42 Cauldon Avenue had plenty of wonderful places to sit. There were two ample plush sofas in the sitting room and a window seat in the conservatory, which gave a stunning view over the modest back garden. The family dining table in the kitchen sat next to the Aga, which pumped out a steady stream of delicious heat day and night. The welcoming kitchen was currently brimming with relatives, come to pay their respects.

To Aero there was nowhere better in the house than here on the ottoman in her bedroom. Her bedroom was a slice of peace and a sanctuary or fun place for her and Lilly to hang out. Today its space acted as a refuge for a different reason, mainly to get away from the sea of endless sad faces, and Aero's own dark thoughts.

Sitting with her knees tight to her chest, Aero felt certain that if she tried to read the same sentence in the open book in front of her one more time, she'd go mad. The words just wouldn't go in, no matter how many times she re-read the text. Even the death of her grandma did not provide an excuse good enough for her to get out of homework for a week or two. Apparently, '*it was good for her to have something to take her mind off things.*' Or so Mum had said.

She loved it here in her bedroom, the perfect spot, nestled underneath the light that crept through the window. Mum and her grandma had spent hours re-decorating the room for her last year. The previous owners had preferred something a little... pinker than her. The new delicate grey and silver paper had a calming effect and gave a feeling of safety and security. There were times when it felt as if the soft light alone almost energised her by its rays, but not today. Today she felt anything other than invigorated. Aero normally felt safer here than anywhere else in the world but now there was something missing. It was all too raw, too painful.

Looking up from the pages of the maths revision book, a shadow just outside the window caught her eye. She did a double take. *Was that... a falcon?* Then she thought, *it can't be.* Real or not, the bird seemed to hover for a second, as it looked at her almost eye to eye, then cocked its head, as if it were looking right inside her. Aero blinked, and both the magic of the moment, and the falcon, were gone.

The smell of something delicious wafted up from downstairs; if she was not very much mistaken, the smell belonged to a pizza. She'd know the sweet aroma of her favourite food anywhere. Despite everything, a smile touched the corners of her lips. *Mum.* She loved how hard her mum tried to cheer her up.

Aero still found herself half-expecting Grandma Joanna just to turn up, thinking she'd bring along something new, one of her tricks to make her smile. Then, like a slap to the cheek, the realisation that she had died flooded into her thoughts. The things you took for granted could disappear in a blink, and then it seemed as if they were never there at all. Except to those who remembered.

Mum had told her that Grandma's heart had given up in the end, that was why she had died, but it seemed impossible. For one thing, her grandmother had been ridiculously healthy. *Perhaps she hadn't noticed Grandma's wrinkles, or time passing through her fingers?* She realised she didn't even know how old her grandmother was. Things like that were never important. Not until they were, like now. She had just been her grandmother. Always was, always would be.

Still, Aero knew her grandmother would soon be nothing more than a half-remembered dream unless she clung fast to her memory. Making a silent vow to the room, Aero promised that she would. She made another promise too. Joanna would not want her to be sad, to stop living. So, she put on a smile, got dressed, and, as far as it could be brushed, tamed her once more unruly hair.

Taking a moment to gather herself, Aero stood outside the kitchen door. She could hear the hum of chatter inside getting louder and louder but could only hear half words and catch phrases that made no sense. Something about terrorists and being exposed. *Too dangerous*. She must have misheard. Ready for the onslaught, Aero entered the kitchen.

"Hello love, you're looking better," Mum announced loudly, making sure everyone knew Aero had arrived. Stifling a nervous giggle, she felt the eyes of the guests on her and the room fell eerily quiet as nobody spoke. No one except Aunt Louise, who in all seriousness and without seeming to realise what she was saying, asked, "How many more have to die to keep our secret?"

A look of panic swept over her mum's face. Aunt Louise was a little deaf, and it sometimes got her into trouble. With practised skill, Mum quickly resumed her composure, and smiled, "Aero, my darling girl. How are you?"

"I'm okay, thank you. What was that you were just saying?"

"Aero!" Mum shouted, as if her question had been a serious crime.

Aunt Louise either didn't hear or chose to ignore her. "Oh, I was just wondering how many more we have to invite to the funeral, dear."

Nodding, Aero knew full well that was not what her aunt had said. She had the distinct impression that everyone in the room knew something apart from her. Fully aware of the tension, she decided against pushing the issue and changed the subject, mostly to ease the obvious look of distress upon her mum's face. "Do I smell pizza?"

"Oh, yes, hun. It's ham, your favourite. Why don't you go and sit in the conservatory and I'll bring some through, hey? We're almost finished here. Just a few last-minute arrangements to decide on."

Aero wished desperately that her mum would realise she wouldn't break hearing them talk about the funeral. Maybe helping them arrange things could even make her feel useful. Still, she did as she was told and left them to it. As she walked away, a lingering feeling stayed with her that her aunt had been trying to tell her something important.

Chapter Eight

*A*ero had found making the decision on whether to go to her grandma's funeral impossible. In the end, her mum had taken the choice out of her hands, stating her indecision as proof she wasn't ready to deal with it. As much as Aero wanted to argue with her, to tell her she felt ready but scared, she found herself unable to make a compelling argument. Especially as she didn't know herself, in truth. Instead, she'd gone to school and pretended the day was just like any other, keeping herself busy and acting as normal as she knew how.

A tiny gnawing voice whispered inside her head, berating her for not wanting to go and visit the gravesite too. Working up the courage by herself seemed unmanageable, but Lilly eased the burden by saying she'd go with her whenever she was ready. Lilly's thinking was that visiting it might help her to come to terms with it all. Closure was the word other adults used to discuss such things, when what they really meant to say was to 'accept it is over.'

Either way, Lilly's kindness had once again proved to her beyond doubt that she truly had the best friend in all the world. Instead of feeling anxious, she found herself looking forward to Lilly coming round. Her friend saw her not as a flaky, immature girl but as someone who only needed love and support. Reassured, Aero felt calm. They would visit together. It would be okay.

All around her life carried on as normal. It had a habit of going on whether you wanted it to or not. Aero supposed the old saying, life is for the living, applied. Or perhaps more accurately, life is in the routine. She'd been back at school for a couple of weeks and trying her best to get on with things. Surprisingly, by her standards, she'd managed to avoid any more trips to the Head's office. Perhaps because, in truth, she couldn't stand the thought of going back there.

There had been a few unexpected surprises though. Take today for instance. Andrew Cole,

the biggest bully and blight on her life had
stolen her pen in science. To which she hardly
shook her head in disbelief, but then he did do
something astonishing. He gave it back and
even managed to crack her a smile. Aero didn't
know if he just felt sorry for her or if maybe
she'd been wrong about him. She wasn't sure,
but one thing she'd come to realise was how
people could have a way of surprising you, and
kindness could come from unexpected places.
She decided to hold off declaring him a saint
just yet, but it had made school better, at least
for today.

The school day over, Aero returned home to
find things there were not so good. A
mysterious tension hung in the air, like an
invisible weight. Aero slipped into the kitchen
for an ice-cold glass of water, leaving her
mum alone in the living room.

Peering at her mum perched on the sofa,
Aero thought she looked older than her forty-
one years. Slumped over, surrounded by cups
of half-drunk tea, she'd aged in these last few
weeks. Having lost weight, her once beautiful
face looked drawn, her eyes tired with the
burden of dealing with her own grief, as well
as that of her daughter. Aero began to realise

the enormous toll her mum had suffered. She supposed the two of them were a pair really, both winging it and pretending in their own way.

She slurped half-heartedly on the drink she hadn't really wanted. She'd only gone to get it as an excuse to escape the weight of grief held in the room.

"Come and sit down, love. There's something we need to talk about." Mum patted the chair next to her, as if to encourage Aero to sit.

Doing as suggested, Aero sat down in the offered seat. There was something unsettling about the strange look on her mum's face. Wringing her hands together, her mum, usually calm and peaceful, seemed agitated. If she didn't know any better, Aero would have thought her confused or anxious about something. Staying silent, Aero wondered if she was about to tell her something. Then her mum picked up a curious looking box from the floor.

"What is it, Mum, you look worried?"

"No, darling, I'm just not sure about something. I'm wondering if this is the right time to give you this or not. You're doing so well settling back into school and everything. The last thing I want to do is upset you again." Mum sucked in a breath between her teeth, chewing at her lip. As if what she had to say could possibly be anything worse than what had already happened.

"Give me what... that?" Aero pointed at the box her mum was gripping tightly in her fingers. A nervous chill ran down her spine. Intuition prompted her to ask, "Is it something of Grandma's?"

"Yes." Mum nodded solemnly. Still clutching the box, she added, "We went to the will reading today, and she left this for you."

Somehow, she'd known it would be from her. Mum handed over the box. Sealed inside black paper, the white label on the wrapping proved it had reached the right person, as Aero saw her grandma's unmistakeable handwriting.

"What is it, Mum? What's inside?"

"I don't know, Aero. Joanna didn't tell me what it contained. I didn't even know she had left this for you until today. We had our... differences."

Raising her eyebrows questioningly, Aero wondered what on earth her mum could possibly mean. It was the first she'd heard of any conflict between them. As far as she knew, Grandma and her mum never argued or disagreed about anything. Before she could ask though, her mum continued, "Erm, we disagreed about whether to tell you something or not."

Exasperated, she yelled, "Mum, you're not making any sense at all! What are you talking about? You argued about me?" She shook her head in disbelief.

"I didn't want to tell you, you see. Grandma did. That's why we argued... what we didn't see eye to eye about. She thought it your right to know and if I'm correct, I'm pretty sure whatever is inside the box, is not only your heritage, but a secret I'm not sure you're ready for. It tells you everything. You need to understand that I've always done what I thought best for you. Aero, love, this may come as a shock."

This time Aero found herself silently holding her breath. Afraid that if she spoke up, the revelation might melt away. She had no idea what her mother was talking about, but it felt like an explanation for many unspoken things between them. Now, it was all about to make sense. Perhaps at last she would be in on the secret.

After a moment, Mum said, "In life you have to make choices about who you're going to be. As your mum, it's part of my job to do that for you until you're old enough to decide for yourself."

"And what about Dad, what does he think about all this?"

"We're a team, Aero, you know that. We've both always done what we thought would be best for you."

Chime. The doorbell rang. "That'll be Lilly. She promised to come with me tonight to visit Grandma's grave."

"Oh, okay. I'll see you later, then. I love you."

It seemed, whether she wanted it or not, the conversation, for now at least, was over. The fleeting chance to find out what her mum had meant to say had also gone. Grabbing her coat, Aero said, "You know, Mum, I'm not as fragile as you think I am. You all have this idea that I'm about to break, but if you could trust me a little, I might surprise you." Closing the door softly behind her, Lilly and Aero headed for the graveyard.

From inside the house, her mum whispered, *"I'm always amazed by you. Be careful."*

Chapter Nine

"What's in the package?" Lilly asked, unsurprisingly curious.

That's when Aero realised that her fingers were still clutching tightly onto the parcel her mum had given her. "This is apparently some huge secret that's going to change my life." Her tone was somewhat sarcastic, tinged with bitterness. *Why had her mother been keeping secrets from her? When would she realise she wasn't a silly little kid anymore.*

Lilly rolled her eyes in a gesture that said she wasn't buying the flippant comment.

Me neither, she thought.

Lilly's eyes fixed on Aero's with a penetrating and unspoken question. *Spill it*, they seemed to say.

Heading away from the house in the opposite direction from school, they strolled on up the long slow hill towards Lake Rode and the parish church, where Joanna had been buried.

"My mum gave it to me, Lilly, but she acted so weird about it. She kept talking about it like it was going to tell me I'm adopted or something. Apparently, Grandma left it to me in her will."

"Well, are you going to open it?" Lilly asked.

"I don't know what to do. Would you?"

The road coiled slowly up and away from home, lined with conifers on either side, quiet and deserted aside from the odd car travelling past. The imposing foliage seemed to emphasise the weight of the box in her hands. Heavier with every step, at last the church came in to view. Despite its age, perhaps because of it, the building had a beauty about it. The colourful stained-glass windows had recently been renovated and the gardens were bursting with spring flowers. In other circumstances Aero and Lilly might have enjoyed the trip.

Though still cool for a spring day, the sun came as a welcome change from the recent wet days. Feeling the weight of Lilly's stare upon her, Aero noted her friend still hadn't answered her question.

The two followed the muddy path around the back of the church and searched out the reason they had come here. Finding Joanna's headstone, Aero absentmindedly leant down to pluck away a couple of carnations that had died from the vase on the grave. As she touched a wilted rose, it seemed to open in front of her, springing back to life. A warm glow passed through her and she felt at peace. It seemed strange to think this could be a place to find comfort.

Did I do that? she wondered. Lilly, still deep in thought, hadn't seemed to notice.

"Why doesn't it say her age, Aero? On the grave. All the others do."

At first, Aero couldn't understand what Lilly was asking. Then, looking around, she noticed her grandmother's headstone which stood at the end of a row with about ten others in the line. Each one had a name and the dates of when the person died, but her grandma's didn't. The inscription on the headstone left her emotional but, like so many things lately, it only brought her more confusion. *'Joanna P Westwood, beloved mother and grandmother. She tricked us until the end and died as she lived, a hero.'*

Aero touched her face, to find it wet with tears. Shrugging her shoulders, and somewhere between laughter and sadness, she replied, "Honestly, I don't think anyone knows how old she was."

"Let's open the package, Aero. Whatever it is, she wanted you to have it. In my book, that makes it pretty special."

Holding the package for a few minutes more, Aero contemplated whether she agreed with her friend. Unopened it held the possibility of hope; the last thing her grandma would ever give to her. Once she committed to ripping open the paper, there would be no more presents, and never again would she receive a surprise from her. The dilemma was a difficult one – the box itself, rather like money in her pocket, burned a hole, intensifying her desire to peek inside it and spend it.

"Shall we?" Aero asked, her tone full of daring. Lilly nodded.

Cautiously, she began to peel back the paper on one of the edges, exposing a wooden box inside the wrapping. It looked pristine and glowed with a deep, rich rosy red colour. Despite its good condition, Aero suspected the wood itself to be old. The box was decorated on the outside with a gold inlay, and within these stripes were some strange-looking symbols.

She didn't have a clue what they meant, having never seen anything like them before. Tracing her fingers delicately over the lines of gold, her hand grew warm. She felt a whoosh of heat pass from its surface, through her fingers and into her body, and almost let go of it.

Aero's heart was pounding heavily in her chest. Lilly's eyes lit up but somehow Aero knew she couldn't sense the box's power as she did. *Whatever is inside, it must be incredible,* she thought. The decision to open the parcel made, her fingers moved all the quicker. Trembling as they grasped the delicate catch and opened the lid, Aero felt both anxious and excited.

She peered nervously inside to see there was a long piece of material. As Aero unravelled it, pulling it out of the box, disappointment swept over her. The material belonged to her grandmother's scarf. How quickly her mood soured. The remaining items in the box included her grandmother's pack of playing cards and a letter. Nothing more. It was frustratingly empty of anything that might explain the surge of power she'd felt holding it.

"That's it? Some secret!" Deflated, Aero put her hands up in the air in despair and looked to her friend. Waves of frustration swept over her, as a pang of disappointment crushed any hopes of understanding to shreds. *I don't know what I was expecting, but this wasn't it.*

"Don't be sad, Aero. Your grandmother must have loved you very much to give you her precious playing cards. You know how much she loved them."

Realising her behaviour might be verging on that of a tantrum and something Lilly couldn't possibly fathom, she pulled herself together. This was exactly the kind of thing which made her mum think she was immature. "Come on, Lilly, let's go home."

Later that night, curled up in the safety of her bed, Aero flicked on her nightlight and opened the letter.

My darling girl,

If you have received this letter, it means I am no longer here. I can only hope this news does not bring you too much sadness, because, Aero, please believe me when I tell you I did not feel ready to leave you. I am an old woman and have lived on this Earth longer than you can contemplate. Although I have many regrets in my life, I fear the worst regrets are those that have not yet come to pass. Because I know I will regret not being able to see you grow up, and not being able to see how wonderful you will become. I fear my biggest regret of all will be not seeing what path you choose to go down. But I do not regret trying to keep you safe, my sweet granddaughter. The things I have done were always for you.

There may be more revelations to come to you, Aero, but for now, I wish to give you my most precious possessions. My scarf, which you can use to wrap away the coldness of this world, and my precious playing cards. Remember, dear, to always have fun! Be mindful though, Aero, these cards are special. Use them wisely, and remember that when the time comes to choose, and make no mistake, this time comes for us all, I know you will do the right thing.

Live full, Aero, squeeze out every morsel, because this existence is long, and this expanse we call life, and everything in between, is there for the filling.

Your grandmother (and all-round amazing magician), Joanna x

Chapter Ten

"As it's Friday tonight, we're going to have a nice family dinner together. Dad should be back from his trip and I know he'll be so happy to see you. We should celebrate. Oh, and you can invite Lilly too if you'd like. After all, she is practically family," Mum announced.

Great, just what she needed, a family dinner. It would be wonderful that her dad would be home again though. She'd missed him and things had been strange since Mum had given her the box. She had been ominously quiet since their conversation, which, though brief, had seemed to hint at something much deeper. She hadn't even asked Aero if she'd opened it, or what was inside. Unusual behaviour from someone who liked to know everything.

At least Friday had finally arrived and tomorrow she would be able to rest. After getting back from the gravesite last night, she'd placed Grandma's box inside her ottoman. She didn't have the energy to look at it then but tonight perhaps she would get it out again. *Maybe it had a secret compartment?* What did the symbols mean? There had to be something more to it.

Aero yawned, thinking back to her sleepless night, wondering what was happening to her. She rubbed at her eyes to remove the caked-up sleep itching at their corners, her whole body aching. Even though she'd not long woken up, her legs jerked and twisted in protest, insisting they hadn't had any sleep. Her head seemed to agree, as the room spun around her. She'd tossed and turned in her bed all night long, her dreams filled with the strangest things. *How much sleep did I get last night?*

She recalled a falcon pecking at bones by Grandma's grave and her playing cards transforming into a person. She had the vaguest idea that someone familiar had spoken to her in the dream, but for the life of her, she couldn't remember the words. It all felt unreal, like something which had happened in the space between being awake and being asleep, half-remembered, half forgotten. Stopping mid-thought, Aero realised her mum was holding out her school bag and waiting for her to answer. "I'll ask Lilly, Mum. Love you."

"Bye sweetheart, have a great day."

How can you do that to me? Please wait, Grandma, I'm coming. You're going to die but I can save you...

"Aero, are you planning on sleeping throughout the entire lesson, or do you want to wake up with a trip to the Head's office?"

Jolting awake, Aero felt the weight of all the eyes of the room upon her. *Oh no, I've been sleeping at my desk.* Mr Bore, her history teacher, loomed over her like a huge shadow, his eyes glaring with anger. Looking away, Aero wondered just how bad it would turn out to be. *Had she been snoring?*

She straightened herself up like someone had shot a ruler up her back and dared to peek around at her classmates. Everyone was staring... at her. She could feel the fiery red flush of embarrassment reaching her ears. Slinking back in the chair, this was one of those moments when she wished the ground would open and swallow her whole.

Great, just great! What was I dreaming about? "I'm so sorry, Mr Bore."

Aero saw Mr Bore's expression had softened. Perhaps he'd been warned she might experience some turbulence. Seeing a look of understanding cross her teacher's face, Aero breathed a sigh of relief. Maybe just this once she would avoid getting in trouble.

"Okay. Well, don't let it happen again."

Thirty minutes later and she was at last free of the torture of the lesson. She dived for the classroom door before anyone else could, unable to bear the thought of hearing everyone laughing at her. Laughing at the girl who had fallen asleep in class.

Just when she thought she couldn't possibly do anything else to embarrass herself, her foot made contact with a loose bit of carpet, throwing the top half of her body forward, and with it her centre of gravity. Tripping, Aero scrambled ungracefully to recover. Tears stung at her eyes, making it harder to see which direction to go in and harder still to cover her tracks. Not daring to looking back, she picked up her feet and set off as quickly as her legs could carry her.

She sprinted to her and Lilly's usual meeting spot by the lockers. Breaking school rules, running through the corridors and across the playground, Aero only stopped once she had reached the safety they seemed to offer. She made it before Lilly got there, and stopped to catch her breath. *At least I should have a few minutes before anyone else gets here,* she thought.

"Snooze and you lose, hey, Aero?" sniggered Andrew Cole, his usual crew behind him, as he purposely knocked into her.

"Hey," Aero replied angrily, rubbing at her shoulder. "How did you get here so fast anyway?" She tried hard not to look at the smirk on his face.

"I guess I was tripping over myself to get here!" Andrew cackled, highly amused by his own joke.

Oh God, he saw that.

Just then, Lilly arrived, somewhat out of breath. Seeing Andrew there, she bravely put herself between them, casting a look that could kill at Andrew. "Are you all right?" she asked. Then she whispered, "You look terrified. Scared right down to the bone, Aero."

"One of those days." She shrugged her shoulders and tried to shrug off the fear too.

"Haven't you got anything better to do than hang around here all day?" Lilly asked.

Knowing he'd done his job in front of his friends, Andrew slinked away guiltily. Aero could still hear his friends laughing far down the corridor. *So much for him being a reformed character. When will this day ever be over?* she wondered. Turning to her friend, she said, "You do know that I love you, Lillith Helena Jones, don't you?"

Lilly's big, kind eyes grew wide and bright beneath her spectacles, and her smile cut through the layers of hurt, burning all the pain away. As the two huddled around their lockers, Lilly whispered, "Back at ya, Aero."

Chapter Eleven

*D*espite the long day, before she knew it she had arrived back home. She knew even before getting inside that her dad had too, because she saw his car back where it belonged in the driveway. It felt like almost everything was getting back to the way it should be.

He opened the front door, greeting her with a warm smile and something of the old twinkle in his eyes. Seeing her made them light up. *It's so good to see his smiling face again*, she thought. Still, Aero couldn't help but notice his face was thinner than before he went away, and despite his smile, he looked sad.

"Dad!" Aero nuzzled into him tightly as he leant forward with open arms. Feeling the prickles of stubble on his usually clean-shaven face, she put her arms around his chest and hugged him instead, not knowing who needed it the most. Since Grandma had gone, she'd carried around this horrible feeling that something bad would happen to him too. She gripped him so tightly he started to cough, and Aero let him go before she broke a rib.

"Good trip?" she asked. She hoped he wouldn't notice the relief in her voice.

"Yes, thank you. Great, but it's good to be home."

He reached inside a carrier bag he held in his left hand. "I picked you up a present."

"Yes!" Aero threw her fists triumphantly in the air. Then she quickly realised with a flash of embarrassment how rude she was being. "Thanks, Dad." The present, a blue unicorn necklace, made the world feel like a better place.

Seeing Lilly standing behind Aero quietly, he added, "And there's one for you too!"

He handed her an identical purple necklace and Aero couldn't help thinking that Lilly had become like the sister she had never had. *Good one, Dad.*

"Lilly, sweetheart, so glad you could make it to dinner. Come on in," Mum chimed in.

Taking her coat, Aero hung it up in the cupboard under the stairs. Before Mum could be all annoying and ask if they wanted anything, Lilly and she escaped to the safety of her bedroom.

"What are we going to do about Andrew Cole?" Lilly asked, plonking herself down on the bed.

"What do you suggest?" Aero replied, snuggling next to her.

"I don't know yet, but something very unpleasant!"

"I agree, Lilly, something truly hideous. Like putting snakes in his bed or spiders in his lunch box." The two giggled outrageously, and just like that, the history class was only a memory.

"Shall we see what YouTube has to offer?" Aero got out her phone and switched it on to their favourite YouTube channel, *Witchcraft.* They both adored watching the magic tricks and trying to figure out how they did it.

"Have you had a chance to try out your grandma's cards, yet?" Lilly asked.

"Nah. It still feels a bit strange to touch them. You know, they wcrc her… thing."

"Maybe we can have a look after dinner?" Lilly asked mischievously, with a glint in her eye. "After all, your grandma wanted you to have them and you never know, it could be fun!"

"Has anyone ever told you you're very persistent, Lilly Jones?"

"Only until I've persuaded them otherwise," she replied, smiling.

Just then Aero saw a flash of inspiration pass across Lilly's face. "I've just had the most amazing idea ever! We could start our own channel and do magic tricks just like your grandma. We could call it something like... learn how to do magic!"

Aero raised her eyebrows and mulled it over for a minute. It wasn't the worst idea she'd ever heard. "I just don't know how to get past it though, Lilly. How do I get over her not being here anymore?"

Before her friend could answer, Mum shouted up, "Dinner's nearly ready. Come on downstairs, please, girls." Aero felt pretty sure the whole street had probably heard and were now headed towards their dinner table.

"Coming, Mum," they shouted together, which set them off in another spiral of giggles and swept away the intensity of the moment. But not before Aero saw a look of understanding on Lilly's face.

No wonder I love her.

The dinner table had been set out with enough junk food to make any teenage girl happy. As Aero's favourite, the pizza was a given, but her eyes lit up at the sight of sausage rolls, egg sandwiches and crisps. She wrinkled her nose at the sight of the fresh leafy salad but knew already she would have to make a token effort to satisfy her mum's need for her to eat healthily. Lilly seemed to know what her friend was thinking as she gave her a knowing look and then laughed. Secretly, Aero felt grateful that dinner would be just for the four of them. She took a seat next to her dad. It really felt good to have him home.

"Oh no. Aero darling, can you pop into the conservatory and get me some tomatoes for the salad? I completely forgot." Without waiting for an answer, Mum handed her a basket. "You're an angel."

Wrapped in a blanket in the wicker chair by the window, Aunt Louise sat with her small hands resting on the arms. Her round chubby face faced away from Aero and looked out onto the garden through the windows. She had a dreamy faraway look she sometimes got, as if inside her head there lived a whole secret world. Aero couldn't help thinking that, despite their differences in appearance, Grandma Joanna and Aunt Louise were very much alike.

The tomato plant rested on the window shelf behind her aunt. Aero coughed loudly enough to make sure she could hear her coming. The last thing she wanted to do was make her jump and scare the life out of them both.

"Hello, Aero dear."

"Hello, Aunty Louise."

Leaning around her ample size, which not only filled the chair but also the corner of the conservatory, Aero picked off three rosy ripe tomatoes and placed them into the basket her mum had given her. Then she stopped and stared at the plant. Only one tomato remained on its small stalks now. Sat in the corner basking in the glow of the sun, plants were something of a hobby of her mum's. She had this single tomato plant and a larger selection of vegetables that she tended to in the garden. Yet, it only just occurred to her that they never ran out of fruit and vegetables. No doubt if she came back tomorrow the plant would be full once again.

"Must be magic or something," Aero muttered under her breath.

"Why yes, of course, dear, that's one of your mother's skills. She is a peregrine magu first class you know," Aunt Louise said proudly.

Aero did a double take at her aunt. Shocked she'd heard her, as her hearing did seem to be selective at times, but even more surprised by her comment. *What on earth is she talking about? Perhaps she'd misheard?*

Staying silent for a moment, Aero thought carefully about what to say next. Maybe now might be the time to ask her aunt about the other strange comments she had made the other day. The ones about people dying. Either Aunt Louise had gone completely mad or she was trying to tell her something. A something that needed her to drop hints. Either way, the time had come to find out.

In order to hide how much she wanted to know what her aunt had meant, Aero put on an airy and somewhat fake voice. "Yes, Mum's a whizz with plants. Totally magical! By the way, the other day, what did you mean when you said how many more will have to die, Aunty Louise?"

"Well it's us and them dear, isn't it? I mean, there's so few of us left now. Someone needs to do something, take a stand. Your poor grandmother. I remember when there were so many of us left and now, well... witchcraft is not what it used to be."

"*Witchcraft?*" Aero asked in a throaty whisper.

She opened her mouth to ask her what the heck she meant when her mum walked in. Obviously, she'd decided to find out where her daughter had got to and why it had taken so long just to pick a few tomatoes. Caught in her mouth, the words were cut off before Aero could get a proper chance to ask her aunt what on earth she had been talking about.

"Come on now, Aero, the food's getting cold, and Aunt Louise, that's quite enough of that sort of talk," her mum said sternly, giving her a stare that could have stripped paint. "Dinner's ready."

Firmly put in her place, Aunt Louise went quiet. Ushered out of the conservatory by her mum, Aero turned on her heels and headed back to the dinner table. Leaving Mum behind with her aunt, Aero knew better than to try and catch wind of their conversation. Still, she chanced a sneaky backwards glance at the tomato plant and gasped. Hanging from the small plant were four fat, juicy tomatoes.

Chapter Twelve

Having finished the rest of the meal without the topic of magical plants being mentioned, Aero sat back in the dining chair and breathed a long, satisfied sigh. "Mum, can Lilly and I be excused, please?"

"Oh yes, I couldn't eat another thing, I'm completely stuffed," Lilly agreed, pushing her plate away.

"Of course. Why don't you two go and amuse yourselves upstairs?"

Aero thought her mother had seemed a little too relieved that the two of them would be out of her way. She couldn't shake the feeling her mother was still trying to keep her away from Aunt Louise. *What is it she's afraid of?* she wondered.

Getting up from her seat, Lilly said, "Thank you for the delicious dinner, Mrs Westwood."

"You're very welcome, Lilly. Any time."

As soon as they were out the door, Aero reached over and gave her friend's arm a friendly but sharp thump.

"Ow, what did you do that for?"

"For being a suck up!"

Lilly stuck her lip out in a pout, then shouted, "Race ya!" With a swift push, she flew past Aero, knocking her against the wall. Despite Aero's best efforts to catch her, Lilly hit the bedroom first by a good couple of strides, grinning wildly as she flopped onto the bed.

"You cheat, Lilly!" Aero protested but her smile said it all.

"So, are we making a video or what?" Lilly asked.

Still catching her breath, Aero eyed up her grandma's cards. Breathlessly, she replied, "I think you might be overlooking one small minor detail, Lilly."

"Oh, what's that?"

"I don't know the first thing about card tricks! How on earth are we going to do a video if I don't even know how to do it?"

As she looked across at Lilly, she saw that she wore a familiar expression, and had a glint in her eye. One she had seen too many times to count. Honestly, there was no arguing with that girl once she got something stuck in her head.

Having managed to distract her friend and keep her happy, the two spent the rest of the night researching and watching videos on how to do basic card tricks. This took a little more practise than Aero had imagined but she had to confess the feel of the smooth cards in her hands felt good.

Soon enough, the time came for Lilly to head home and as much as she'd enjoyed her company, Aero was ready to have her own space again. Being sociable felt exhausting; her head and heart needed time to heal. It wasn't so much having to put on a fake smile, especially with Lilly, who she felt the most comfortable with in all the world, it was more that being happy felt like a betrayal.

Her thoughts always seemed to run the same way. How could she enjoy herself without her grandma around? How could she be happy when she should be feeling sad? Aero slumped down on the bed and in only moments the waking world slipped away as sleep found her.

Grandma!

Aero woke with a start. Gasping for breath, she pulled in large gulps of air. Sitting up, she could tell from the lack of light it was still early. She glanced over at the alarm clock on her bedside table, its soft green light showing 5:13 am. She'd been dreaming again; she vaguely remembered the purple and gold thread from her grandmother's scarf, but the rest had mostly become a blur. Thinking hard, trying to recall the details, Aero had the strangest feeling her aunt had been in the dream this time too. *Weird.*

Brr. Wrapping the duvet around her, she tried to plug the holes to keep out the cold air, but the hairs on the back of her neck stood up to attention. *Well, there's no point trying to get back to sleep now. What the heck.* Still wrapped up, she leant across and flipped on her lamp, then reached for the cards.

Zap! A jolt of electricity sparked as she reached out for them. *Damn static.* Even as she said it, she knew that wasn't quite right. *Something else.* The cards seemed to be sending out an unseen vibration. Aero sensed they had an energy all of their own.

Remembering how her grandma used to hold them, her fingers tingled with anticipation. She placed the pack in her hands. As she slipped them out of their case, she felt a warm throb pulse through her. Reflected in the mirror, her face gleamed bright with knowledge. It was as if Grandma had known, almost as if... there was a thought on the tip of her tongue, but she couldn't quite put it into words.

Still, something inside her urged her on. Shuffling through the cards, Aero focused on the moves she had watched with Lilly on the videos earlier that night. A warm cushion of air wrapped around her. Or perhaps she simply stopped noticing the cold as her fingers began to move by themselves, cutting the pack into two halves. Once again, she could feel the power pulsing off them, as if they had already known what to do and had been simply waiting for the right person to come along. Feeling energised, she reached for her phone camera.

Dare I try?

Holding on to her composure, she switched on the mobile phone video to record. She started filming and began to try a trick with the cards. Tentative at first, she felt the power building around her. So absorbed in the task was she, Aero didn't see the light around the cards begin to bend, and she didn't notice the aura that now surrounded her.

On their favourite YouTube channel, '*Witchcraft*', they used a variety of props and the magic of editing to do the tricks. Yet Aero knew in this moment, she didn't need any of them. As her fingers jumped around, she could already see the moves needed inside her mind.

She imagined the cards flipping into the positions she wanted, racing through the air, unaware they were responding solely to her thoughts now and not her fingers. She kept at it, performing trick after trick. Encouraged to push further with each success, the cards began to hum and a slick bead of sweat dropped into her eyes. Suddenly, a cold chill swept over her. She felt afraid.

What am I doing?

Focus. The voice inside her head rang out crystal clear, but it sounded unfamiliar. Terrified, she dropped the cards as if they were on fire, but the feeling of someone else being in the room, inside her head, lingered on. The temptation to run became almost overpowering, but what would her parents think? She would only terrify them with ramblings of talking cards and show them she was exactly what they already thought: a hysterical teenager. Besides, something just as strong told her this moment could change her life. This was destiny. If only she could open her mind to it. Shuddering as she pulled the covers back around her, she resolved never to look at the video she had taken.

Chapter Thirteen

*P*erri's footfalls were wearing a deep groove into the carpet. Pacing, she just couldn't seem to stay in one place, to settle. It didn't matter how many cups of tea she had, nothing could calm her. Since Joanna's death, every noise threatened to send her over the edge and this waiting wasn't making things any easier.

Xander had thought Louise coming to the house would help her but it only made things worse. Perri's sister had always been the more talkative and outspoken of the pair. Louise believed Aero ought to know about Joanna. She thought they were making a mistake not telling her about her murder, about their magic, and well... about everything. But how could they tell their daughter that her grandmother had been murdered, and she was in peril now too? It was hard enough for them living with the fear every day. They couldn't inflict the anguish of this knowledge onto Aero as well.

Aero had always been sensitive and felt things more acutely than others. This had only been made worse by their constant drifting lifestyle. Her daughter didn't need to look for evidence she didn't fit into this world as others did, Aero experienced reminders every day. Perri had seen how Aero had wrestled with whether to go to the funeral or not. She couldn't imagine telling her the truth. There was no way she would cope. She was just a girl, a mortal one at that. As far as Perri was aware she'd never shown the slightest magical aptitude at all.

Her daughter had been blessed with many other wonderful talents which made Perri's heart fill with pride, she didn't need magic to be special. Aero deserved a chance to explore all the extraordinary things being ordinary had to offer. Since they had settled in Cranage her artistic side had blossomed. She had real flair when it came to the use of different materials in her artwork. They were settled here in Cauldon Avenue and Aero had even managed to make a friend, a best friend. It made her happy. Or she had been before all of this happened.

Perhaps it was why they'd stayed so long and ruined everything. *Was it all her fault? Is this why her mother had died?* Aero wasn't the only one who wrestled with difficult decisions. Perri had been the one to persuade the family to stay, because all the running had made life impossible for them all, not least her daughter. Aero had been isolated and friendless. *It had to stop, didn't it?* Caught in a relentless, vicious cycle, placing all the blame on her own shoulders, she truly believed she was the cause of Joanna's death. Still, it broke her heart to think of breaking up their lives and moving yet again. She couldn't take Aero away from Lilly, the only thing helping to keep her daughter going, but when would it all end?

"Shall I make us another drink?" Louise asked, sliding her head out from behind the kitchen door, as if using it as a shield.

"I'm drowning in tea," Perri snapped. Her eyes skirted first to the coffee table, then the sideboard, finally landing on several half-cmpty cups.

"Well, there's no need to bite my head off, now is there!" Instead of retreating into the safety of the kitchen, Louise came out and began to collect up the cups.

"I'm sorry Lou-lou, I'm just so on edge. What time did they say they were coming?"

"Eleven o'clock," Xander chimed in. Rather than wearing a groove in the carpet, Xander appeared to have grown one in his face. The deep-set crease between his eyes turned into a ridge as he sat hunched over in the arm chair, his hands propping up his head.

"You're not exactly helping, you know, Louise," Perri said.

Perri noticed Xander raise an eyebrow at this which flattened out the worry lines in his face temporarily.

"Oh?" Louise whispered. She'd dumped the cups in the kitchen sink, and taken refuge behind the sofa.

"No. All this talk of magic to Aero. Loose tongues are dangerous, Louise, you know that."

"But the girl needs to know, Perri. She's in danger, whether she knows it or not. You're not doing her or you any favours by keeping her in the dark. You might well be the older sister, Perri, but sometimes I think you forget what they did to me." Louise pointed at her ears. "That brings a certain clarity to a situation, Perri. I know exactly how dangerous they can be, and I know how scared you are. But none of it changes a damn bloody thing. They'll still come after us whether we're frightened of them or not. Preparation is the key and the girl needs to be ready!"

Perri had at last found a spot to stay in, albeit perched on the front of a cushion. Between them came a long pause, followed by a longer silence. Her face was contorted with the despair she felt inside. Her sister had the good sense not to push the matter any further. Instead, she came out from behind the chair and sat down next to her.

"Do you think Aero is okay?" Perri asked. Rather than wait for an answer she checked her watch. She was anxious, there were still five minutes before the man they were waiting for was expected to arrive. "I'm just going to pop out, I won't be a minute."

Knowing better than to argue, Xander and Louise stayed mute as Perri headed to the kitchen and pushed open the window. Her eyes closed, she mumbled,

Forces of nature, as one with me,
Wings of a falcon, be me, be free.
Dance in the night, sing in the day,
Be with me, be one now, I pray.

Without a fanfare or flash of lightning, but with only an almost imperceptible bending of the air, she transformed into a peregrine falcon. The rapid process took less than a second. Her long slender fingers were replaced with flexible wings. At the end of her legs were sharp, knife-like talons. The sunlight through the open window bounced off her steely focused eyes, reflecting specks of yellow and honey. Those penetrating eyes were now fixed on their objective. She stretched, testing their strength, then took flight on her confident wings. Perri launched out of the window and went in search of her daughter.

Chapter Fourteen

*L*ouise and Xander sat in silence opposite one another. Without any magical ability of his own, the 'magic gene' being passed down solely on the female side of the Westwood family, Xander sometimes found himself on the outside, as much as he liked Louise and loved his wife. With nothing to do but wait for Perri's return, an awkward void existed between them, desperate to be filled. Louise, normally the talkative type, sat oddly silent.

Xander found both were equally annoying and loveable in their own way but each had qualities he admired. Still, without the shared experience of magic, and aside from Aero, they lacked anything in common. Xander felt it now more than ever. Like any other husband and father, he felt the drive to protect his family, but here he was, powerless against an unseen entity whose sole purpose existed to eliminate those he loved. It felt like having the knowledge of a truck hurtling towards him without any brakes, standing directly in its path. Logic told him to move, but nonetheless his feet were planted firm and wouldn't budge. It rendered him petrified and helpless.

"Can you please explain what in the hell just happened with your wife? When is the damn woman going to listen to reason?" Louise said, finding her voice at last.

"Erm, I could ask you the same question?" Xander whispered. Then more loudly, "Funny how she's always my wife and not your sister whenever you disagree with her."

"Hmm," Louise grunted. "I just wish you could get her to see sense, Xander, for all our sakes. Surely you can see the madness in these secrets? Aero needs to know."

"I think you'll find I agree with my wife in all things. She's always right, even when she's wrong," Xander replied, giving Louise a fixed stare to put an end to the discussion.

For the second time that day, Louise knew she could not push the subject further. *Perhaps she would take matters into her own hands instead?* Perri had become blind with grief, so much so she could not see that her daughter was coming of age, but she saw it. She had already tried to hint at the girl about the possibilities.

Louise's way to deal with the sorrow was much like her mother's attitude to living. Grab it, tackle it head on and run from nothing, not even sadness. Being the younger of the two, Louise had fought for attention all her life. Joanna had loved them both of course, but in a family of three witches, when you came last, the odds were automatically stacked against you. Whatever the man from the government said today would be irrelevant. Louise would not rest until she had found the murderer and got her revenge, with or without her sister's help. As for the girl, she would not let her niece go through the perilous puberty of a witch all by herself.

Lost in her thoughts, Louise found herself unusually quiet. She suddenly noticed that Xander was watching her intently. Realising the air had become weighted with anticipation, she decided to try a different tact. "Your parents, are they well?"

"As far as I know. I haven't spoken to them in months."

"I'm sorry, Xander. I guess you didn't sign up for all this, hey? When you married Perri, you kind of married the whole clan!"

"I wouldn't have it any other way. Well, perhaps if I could choose, but it's best I don't contact them. There's no trail that could lead back to them, you know. They're safe, which is what counts."

Before they could continue the doorbell chimed, followed swiftly by a whoosh and a gentle hum. Perri had returned.

"Is she okay?" Xander asked Perri.

Louise saw Perri give a swift nod before promptly striding across the living room to the front door to get on with the matter at hand. Magical defence charms were set as part of routine in the Westwood house. She released them now by moving her hand in an arc behind the door, and then unlocked it with the key. Perri took a step back as the heavy set, wooden panelled door opened inward.

"Mrs Westwood," the man said.

The words were a statement, rather than a question as to her identity. The man, dressed in a soft black leather jacket, starch white tennis shoes and flat cap, looked nothing at all like they'd expected.

Perri had assumed he would be a James Bond look alike, or at the very least, a man in a suit. *Just goes to show,* she thought. Sensing her confusion, the man flipped out a plain black leather wallet and proved his identity with his government issue credentials.

"Please come in," Perri said, sweeping her arm in a welcoming gesture.

Brushing past her as he entered, the man recoiled slightly at their nearness. His wide blue eyes took in everything in the room. His shoes squeaked slightly on the wooden floor.

Please take a seat, Mr...?"

"Chambers, Maxwell Chambers. Thank you. What a lovely home," he remarked politely. Although he measured his voice carefully, his top lip was pulled back in an expression Perri couldn't place. *Fear, anger?* She didn't know.

"Would you like some tea, Mr Chambers?"

Louise tittered mildly underneath her breath. Perri shot her a glance that could kill.

"Oh no, that's quite all right. There's no need to run around after me. I'm sure you'd prefer to be getting on with other things."

Perri couldn't settle on a tone of voice and bounced around between polite and frenzied, terrified of what this man might be about to tell them. Unsure if he was afraid of them or angry.

Her mother had always taken care of this side of things. She'd been their protector and the diplomatic one. Perhaps because she'd had so much practise being peacemaker between her and Louise when they were kids. Still, it did no good to dwell on the past. Their whole future pivoted on this point, this meeting. Whether to stay or whether to leave their home in Cranage.

"So, what have you got to tell us. Have you found the men responsible?" Perri asked.

"We're continuing our investigation but the Real Worlders are slippery. It seems they've gotten more organised in their old age."

"Old age?" Perri enquired, puzzled.

"I expect your mother filled you in?"

Their faces blank, the trio stayed silent.

"I can tell you a little, but I'm afraid most of the details are a matter of clearance."

"Yes, understood, Mr Chambers."

"Our unit was formed back in the day to keep an eye on the so-called 'conspiracy theorists' to assess the potential for criminal activity in relation to military intelligence and ensure the defence of the country. When I say unit, I mean to say just the one person, because these folks were disorganised at best and the threat minimal. Bluster mainly. Most of their theories had enough truth in them to make them feel they knew what they were up to but not enough for them to cause any real damage. As you can probably gather, it was our man's job to drip feed just the right amount of information. The Internet, however, has made it a different game, and so our unit expanded. More undercover ops. More folks on the inside. As these groups began to organise themselves better, so too did the information they collected. One group branched off and became what we now know as the Real Worlders. Until this point, we'd had no idea you existed. That, of course, all changed."

"Yes, that much we do know," Perri offered.

"As you are aware, this terrorist cell, and I don't use the term loosely, has been hunting your kind down. We were working with your mother on some new information we'd received. She wasn't supposed to engage with them. It was purely reconnaissance. But I don't have to tell you how stubborn Joanna could be. Unfortunately, there it goes cold."

Perri shot him a glance. How could he be so heartless, with their own mother cold in her grave.

"The trail, I mean. They've gone into a black hole, literally. They've completely disappeared and there's no trace of them, not even on the dark web. I'm afraid I can't say any more, except that I think it would be in your best interests to relocate. If they identified your mother, then they know who you are."

Louise said, "In other words you have no idea who killed our mother and what they are up to?" Perri took no offence at her sister's interruption, for she too had been thinking exactly the same, but perhaps would not have been brave enough to say it.

"I would like to suggest otherwise but I don't want to give you false hope. I'm not at liberty to tell you any more, except to say that I've already told you more than I should."

Louise pressed on. "And this has nothing to do with the potential for weapons? Surely your unit could make use of a witch or two? All this time, I assume you've been watching us too? Isn't that right, Mr Chambers?"

Perri observed Maxwell Chambers closely. The poor guy seemed ill prepared for their onslaught, young as he was. Perhaps he was also equally unprepared for how close to the mark they would come. She guessed they'd hit the nail on the head, that they were indeed being watched, and he had obviously been put in charge of making sure they were not a threat.

He seemed to struggle to maintain his composure, his arms crossed tight across his chest, afraid to let down his protective barrier. It was clear from his manner he feared the thought of witches running rampant. Perhaps he worried about the damage they might do to the defence of the country. His ignorance shone out as clearly as if they were black and back in a time of racial prejudice. Whatever he had been expecting, sitting here in their home was evidently unnerving for him.

Drawing a deep breath, Chambers deflected the question. "I understand emotions are running high, but our only goal is to prevent these terrorists from causing any more damage. I can assure you we are doing everything we possibly can. I will let you think things over, and if you decide to move on, my team can sort out all the paperwork. New passports, identities as needed, and of course, this incident will be kept out of the papers. The Real Worlders have done the job for us for the most part, eradicating the most bothersome of the witches. Still, I'm under no illusions, the public are ill prepared for the realities of magic. The country is not prepared for a war. I will keep the peace."

"We shall not be running again, Mr Chambers," Perri answered defiantly.

"Very well, I understand. I shall have my team post surveillance then, protection for you. I ask at the very least you inform us if you have any contact with these terrorists. Under no circumstances are you to go after these people on your own. Will you agree to that, Mrs Westwood?"

"Of course, Mr Chambers," Perri replied.

Perri chose reflection and contemplation over words, whilst her sister had always traditionally been the louder of the two. This careful dance between Mr Chambers and them was no gentle waltz. She had seen the look of recognition in his eyes as Louise had asked them if they too were being watched. They would not run but perhaps there was more than one enemy to be found here? Only time would tell.

Chapter Fifteen

"Ready for this?" Lilly asked. The two girls sat down close to the back of the packed school hall and tried hard to ignore the smell; an odour that could only be described as a room full of sweaty students.

"Hardly. I wonder what's in store for us this week," Aero replied.

At best, school assemblies were designed as a test of endurance. An hour-long session listening to another lengthy and mind-numbing list of announcements and achievements, being forced to clap for the successes of other far more talented children, and essentially trying to stay awake.

At worst, this was when the school would spring some new initiative upon them. One with which they were all forced to comply, to demonstrate respect and responsibility, or some such nonsense. Today though proved to be somewhere in between. First came the usual tedious announcements, then the mention of a residential trip, and then finally a thing that neither Aero or Lilly registered that the pupils had to get involved with. It was the thing in the middle, the residential, that had Aero and Lilly excited and nervous in equal measure.

"They're sending us camping?" Lilly asked. Her eyes twinkled with excitement.

"The only place I like to go camping is in a hotel. With a hot bath, a proper bed and a toilet that hasn't been used by fifty other people that morning," Aero replied.

Not to be deterred by Aero's lack of enthusiasm, Lilly said, "It could be fun though, couldn't it? If we're together?"

"I suppose, but what exactly is a yurt?" Aero asked.

"No idea, but I'm sure we'll find out!"

"Listen, I got to run to class, Lilly. Coming?"

"I've just got to get my book from my locker. Besides, I'm off to music on the other side. Catch up with you at lunch?"

"Will do!"

Aero didn't like walking around the school by herself, but she'd reached the age where you were supposed to be confident and unworried by such things. Tag teams were for newbies, not children of her age. Still, she kept her head down and strolled purposefully across the playground, trying desperately to shake the feeling that something bad was about to happen. She headed on to her next destination in the art department, located in the annexe behind the three-story Parker building.

Walking out across the playground, the only way to reach it, she went around the back of Parkers and in through the walkway, which led to the extension. They called it that but really it was a classroom made from a portacabin. Pool House Secondary School hadn't quite caught up with the modernising trend. Still, what the art department lacked in aesthetics, it amply compensated for with the enthusiasm and skills of its teachers.

Intensely aware of the sounds of her own breathing, Aero pushed on across the playground, but trouble loomed ahead of her in the form of Andrew Cole and his friends. Breaking into a half-walk, half-jog, Aero avoided giving them any eye contact, and did her best not to let her own imagination run away with her. *They're not after me. They're just there. If I can't see them, they can't see me,* she thought, and kept on moving.

At the back of the building where it met the end of the canteen, the walkway narrowed. Aero did her best to pretend that Andrew Cole and his friends weren't lining up deliberately to block her path. Still, she felt the trickle of her own cold sweat running down her back and her heart pounded heavily in her chest. Glancing behind her, Aero realised the horrible truth – she was alone.

"You want to watch where you're going, in case you trip up again," Andrew said.

He put his arm up in a gesture that told her she wasn't getting past them without a fight. Stopping, because she had no choice, Aero kept her eyes to the ground and did her best to ignore them. A tactic she already knew wouldn't work but she could hardly fight a group of them.

"Where's your little playmate?" Andrew asked.

"Looks like you're all alone," crowed the rest of the group.

The air around Aero began to feel tingly and heavy. It reminded her of being small and afraid. How she had curled up in her mother's arms and trembled at the thought of a storm on its way. She'd always known it was coming long before the thick clouds would appear. Yet the sky had been clear and crisp this morning with no sign of a storm. This was a different kind of trouble brewing.

"Why don't we have a look in your bag and make sure you've got everything you need? Wouldn't want you to turn up for class without the right equipment." Andrew turned to the rest of his crew, his mouth pulled into a sneer. "What else are friends for?"

Aaron snatched the backpack from her shoulder and tore at the zip. He tipped it upside down with a jerk and the contents spilt out onto the concrete of the playground floor. Aero watched in slow motion as her pencil case bounced on one corner, splitting open, and sent her precious art pencils flying out in all directions.

"Oh dear, oh dear, oh dear," chimed Mara in a singsong voice. "What have we here? This will never do. You're going to end up with a bad mark turning up to class like that."

Aero slipped her hands inside her coat pocket. Feeling a surge of anger swell through her body, she clenched her fists tightly. It felt as if the storm she'd sensed coming had actually been brewing inside her. The anger at hearing the news of her grandmother's death had given her the same feeling. Now those emotions bubbled up close to the surface. Her fingers brushed against something smooth and familiar. The playing cards. Funny, she didn't remember putting them in her coat. Regardless, all at once she felt connected to her grandma again. A surge of electricity rushed through her and her skin burned with strength.

Snatching her hands out of her pocket, Aero raised them, as if they were weapons, in Andrew Cole's direction. She concentrated the anger inside her and felt it burst through her fingers in his direction. For a moment, Aero stood gasping for breath from the exertion. Out of the corner of her eye she spied movement, which was closely followed by a loud thud. Only then did she dare to look up. Andrew had been flung backwards and had landed on the floor. Red droplets of blood dripped from his nose. *Had she done that?* Aero glanced down at her hands in disbelief. On the outside they looked normal and unchanged. She readied for a second round, not daring to relax her guard. Waiting for revenge to strike her, Aero counted her breaths, as if counting the beats between lightning strikes. Scrabbling to his feet, Andrew got up off the floor.

"What the hell?" he muttered under his breath. Clutching his bloody nose, his eyes were wide with fear. Aero realised in a flash that he was terrified of her. Panic swept over her and she quickly lowered her arms. Her body shook with a mixture of relief, pride, and fear of herself. Instinctively, she reached into her pockets again, feeling for the cards. Their smooth surface calmed her, as Andrew and his crew scarpered in the other direction.

Bending down, she collected up her belongings and stuffed them back inside the backpack. The zip broken, she clutched it tightly in front of her. Noticing how eerily quiet the day seemed, she set off for her lesson. Still, she trembled and walked on rubbery legs.

Chapter Sixteen

A far cry from the usual bubbly Westwood meals, dinner that evening saw everyone eating in silence. If they noticed Aero's lack of conversation they didn't say. It seemed their thoughts were elsewhere. *Which was just as well*, Aero thought. She'd managed to run upstairs undetected and hide the broken bag straight after school. How long it would remain hidden she wasn't sure but for now at least, she didn't have to tell them about the 'incident.' She wouldn't have a clue where to start.

Later that same night, Aero lay on her bed and stared up at the dark ceiling. It looked black and unfamiliar, as if it held some secret which might consume her. Her bedroom didn't offer the usual sanctuary she found there and instead felt claustrophobic. The homely gentle aroma of freshly washed clothes and the soft fabrics of the bed sheets had been replaced with the smell of stale sweat and her own fear. The only alternative would be to face the awkward silence downstairs, but Aero had a funny feeling that if she dared to leave the bedroom, she would become their talking point. Not something she wanted to encourage at all.

Running away is not always a speedy endeavour. Instead, sometimes, it is a slow retreat. Aero curled up into a ball and hid herself away from the world. It was a feeling of being stuck between a rock and a hard place. A desperate attempt for her to avoid thinking about the things in her life that she couldn't understand. Sometimes, running away was as simple as hiding from the things that terrify you the most.

A light tap at the door interrupted her thoughts and made her jump. She'd tried hard to be quiet and feign sleep. Obviously, someone had decided to take their chances. When the door didn't open, she realised it couldn't be her mum. Mothers, especially hers, were good at partial privacy but seemed to lack the commitment to follow through. Hence, whenever her mum knocked on the bedroom door, she didn't wait to be invited in but instead waltzed right on in. Whoever stood on the other side of her door paid an unfamiliar courtesy.

"Who is it?" Aero asked tentatively.

"It's me, Aunt Louise. Can I come in, hun?"

Aero sloped off the bed, flicked on her lamp and opened the door. "Sure, come on in."

Aunt Louise took a seat on the ottoman and placed a tray next to her.

"I thought you might like a cuppa. It's herbal tea. My own blend, I brought the herbs with me," she said proudly.

"Thank you," Aero replied. She eyed the cup dubiously, then took a small and suspicious sip of the cloudy liquid.

"Wow, it's actually pretty good," she replied, unable to hide the genuine surprise in her voice. Her aunt's lips curled into a proud smile.

"It's calming. Thought you might need it. You looked as white as a sheet at dinner. Your mum, as you know, has the knack with growing things. I guess you could say herbs arc mine. By the way, did you ever ask your mum and dad how it is you got to be called Aeronwen?"

Somewhat taken aback by the question, Aero shook her head. "Bad sense of humour?"

"It means blessed one, and you are, my darling girl. You are blessed."

Aero laughed nervously, trying to think of some quick retort to throw to her aunt. *Why the tea? Did she know what she was thinking?*

"Fear is like a rope, Aero. We hold on to it, scared of letting go, but the thing about the rope is it's really an anchor in disguise, keeping us tethered, unable to move, unable to break free. Tell me, my sweet girl, what is it you're afraid of?"

Aero's face contorted with the conflict she felt inside. As she mulled over the words, her aunt sat quietly sipping from her cup, as if she had all the time in the world. It seemed clear to Aero that her aunt didn't want to push her, and her kind gesture was a way to cover up how much she wanted to help. She thought again that something was holding her back, for some reason, her aunt's hands were tied. Perhaps she was worried it would be too dangerous for her?

Just then, Aero spotted a quizzical look come over her aunt's face. If she didn't know better, she would have thought her aunt could see something in herself that she could not yet understand. Unbeknown to her, a magical aura flowed from her skin with a rich powerful glow that lit up the whole room around her.

"Did you like the box your grandma left you?" Aunt Louise asked.

Once again, the question surprised Aero. "Yes, although it's strange."

"Maybe you could try googling the symbols. You're a bit of a whizz at this computer malarkey, I understand? Grandma Joanna always said so. Perhaps they have some root in artistry. You could try to find out?"

"How do you know about the symbols?" Aero asked.

This time it was her aunt's turn to remain silent. Instead, she collected the cups and got up.

"Well, I'll leave you to get some rest. Just remember, trust can ease the pain and it's love that makes us courageous. You are blessed, and you are loved, Aero. Always."

Acro leant on her window sill and gazed out into the night. The soft glow of her lamp cast shadows into the back garden. Her window looked out over their small patch of grass, and in the daytime she could see everything. It could hardly be considered a garden to be proud of but in the spring, the one large tree, a cherry blossom, cast out its luscious flowers and flooded it with a carpet of colour, turning it into a magical place.

Past the trees and gates to the rectangular space next to the vegetable planters, the other houses encroached. Behind that, the road that led out of the village connected her with the outside world and to all that lay beyond. She always felt safe and happy looking out on to the world. From here, she was an onlooker to all its beauty and protected from its dangers.

In the eerie shadowy glow, usually Aero could see little else but the boxy shapes of the street lights in the distance and the outline of the tree. Its branches stretched out far across the other gardens, as if to say it would not be contained, that growth was inevitable. Gates and fences were irrelevant, no barriers of the human world would hold it back.

But tonight, it seemed her eyes saw anew. The world and darkness no longer held any fear. She could pick out so much vivid detail, as if someone had switched on all the lights inside her head. She could see the individual blades of grass moving in the soft night time breeze, the smallest insects crawling and even the worms wiggling underneath the surface of the soil. She rubbed her eyes in disbelief. Everything had changed. The same Earth stood beneath her feet, but it felt to her as if the universe was no longer the same place.

She supposed the way to describe the feeling might be like describing the difference between a photograph of a place and being there. It was all the things you couldn't see, the depth, which brought everything to life. The smells, the sights and sounds. Inexplicably, all she knew was that she felt different and it felt good.

Turning her attention back to the evening's odd conversation with her aunt, she thought about what she had heard. She had to ask herself why she should even care about her grandmother's box and its silly symbols. Grandma Joanna had left, abandoning her, and leaving her with no need to cling to a memory.

Aero reached for her grandmother's scarf and held it tight to her chest. The sweet floral scent of her perfume lingered on the material.

No, the box and the cards had been left to her for a reason. Joanna had wanted her to have them.

Closing her eyes, she remembered that her grandmother had always seen the best in her. She'd always seen the true her, the potential of what she could be; holding the scarf, Aero knew that her belief remained. She was trying to tell her something and she would listen.

Aero thought back. Her grandmother had once told her that the world was a big place but the people in it think small. They focus their attention on the little things. What they want, what they can get, how you look, how much stuff you can remember. But they have things backwards, they should be thinking big and seeing the world as a smaller place. She'd told her, the small things they did were the most important. Having each other, family, kindness. People, she had told her, would do horrible things for the big world they live in. Grandma said it was small people like Aero who would be the ones to change it. When she talked, Aero listened because she always told the truth.

What about what happened today? She knew she had secrets of her own now; the strange things in her life, the new powers. Whatever was happening to her was real. Her family and Aunt Louise knew something about them. So why didn't her aunt just tell her? What other reason could there be for the unexpected visit?

The answer seemed obvious; for some reason she couldn't, but she had hinted at clues. Her ability with herbs, her mother's talents for growing things. The tomatoes. Did they all have talents? Was that the big secret?

Aero put down the scarf, and with it cut the ropes that had been holding her back. No more running, no more retreating. Flipping open the laptop, she began the search for answers.

Chapter Seventeen

S tuffing a blanket underneath the doorway to cut out the light, hoping everyone would assume she was still fast asleep, Aero began to work. She regularly looked up things like information, pictures or books on her laptop for a school project. The Internet really was an amazing place but searching for a set of obscure symbols was like looking for a needle in the biggest haystack she could imagine. What would she search for, what was the topic?

After over an hour of trawling through hundreds of artists, she concluded that, whilst they were all no doubt hugely talented, she had got nowhere. The search was impossible! Only then did she notice the stillness of the house. Everyone else had gone to bed. Sneaking downstairs, painfully aware of her clumsiness, Aero navigated successfully to the kitchen and prepared herself a tray of cookies and a hot chocolate. Chocolate made everything better. She needed to feed her brain and she could think of no better way.

Aero took out the pack of playing cards and held them in her hand. The box her grandmother had left her had to be old. Maybe even an heirloom, hence why her grandmother had left it to her. Her aunt had hinted at artistry. Something old and artistic. Her aunt should seriously have given her a better clue. Did she have any idea how many artists there were in the world, both dead and alive? Aero munched on another cookie and wrapped her fingers around the cup of hot chocolate. As she inhaled the delicious sweet smell, she felt the fog in her brain begin to lift. The information in her mind shuffled around rather like the playing cards... historic, something artistic, and symbols.

She typed old historic symbols into the search engine and found herself rewarded with hundreds of images. Nazi symbols, Greek, even witchcraft. Her family had nothing to do with Hitler, that much she felt sure of, but times like these made her wish she had paid more attention to her mother. She was always going on about their family history. Who had married who, where they grew up. Aero had to be honest, she'd thought it all boring and pointless until now. Most of the time, history sounded something like a foreign language to her. Even her own family's seemed alien to her.

What are you, what do you mean? she whispered into the computer.

Maybe she just needed something more to narrow down the search. She added the words, herbs and Westwoods. There! She almost shouted out loud, and then remembered that everyone else was still sleeping. On the box from her grandma, each of the symbols were subtly different. Yet each of them had one part, which looked the same. A foundation of some sort that all the others grew from. This base symbol on the cards caught her eye. On the screen in front of her was something that looked similar but not exact. Still, it gave her more than enough. A glimmer of hope.

Aero clicked on the picture and saw a link too. Following the trail of breadcrumbs, feeling more like a detective in a hunt to solve a great mystery than a girl, she started to read the information, but the hot chocolate and the lateness of the hour were catching up with her. It started off slowly, her eyes staying shut just a fraction longer than she wanted them to. Then they began to water, making it harder to read the words in front of her, until all too soon, they refused to open. She placed her head down on the keyboard and a few seconds later, the house was once again still. Quiet, except for the gentle sounds of her snoring.

Chapter Eighteen

*I*n an unremarkable location a gathering was taking place. The room had been prepared for a conference and the attendees were due to arrive shortly. One woman had arrived early to the venue to prepare. Having first swept the floor and sprayed an entire bottle of air freshener into the room, she placed a total of thirteen red plastic chairs around a fold-up table. At the head of the table, she hooked her bag over the chair facing the others. Out of it, she took a pack of pens and set up a whiteboard behind her. On it, she drew up a crude map that showed the locations of Cauldon Avenue, and the surrounding area. Taking her red whiteboard pen, she lightly inhaled the scent and smiled. She wrote a single word above the map: Westwoods.

The woman settled into her chair, quiet and still, as the guests began to enter from the door at the back. In truth, she would have preferred a more auspicious location for such a momentous occasion, but it would have to do. Inside, the walls were grubby and stained with old stale smoke. Once upon a time this had been a club for working men to gather but it had been a long time since anyone had used either the room or the building. Outside, the unlit road was pot-holed and uncared for, but need prevailed over the lack of luxury on this occasion.

She reached into her bag once more and pulled out a piece of chewing gum. Those of a superstitious nature might have been worried by the number of guests due to arrive but not Megan. They didn't need luck, they had truth on their side. They were fighting an unseen war, played out in the shadows. History wouldn't know about the heroes in this room, but she would. They were saving humanity. She would save it. That was reward enough.

When everyone had sat down, the room went still. Megan stood up and began to address the participants. "Well, colour me impressed. I'm so glad you all could make it this far. I know it's a bit out of the way and hard to reach. Truly, it warms my heart, it does. Gives me hope for humanity. Now, I know we'd all like to be meeting in a nicer location but perhaps it's not a bad thing we're here today. Because if they," she pointed at the whiteboard behind her, "start running things, then this is the kind of life we'd have to get used to. Humans, the non-magical kind would be second class citizens. So, look around my friends, breathe it in. Stale sweat, the smell of humanity's loss. Take it in and remember this moment."

Murmurs of agreement echoed around the space.

"The Westwoods are a plague. They have the kind of power that could destroy us all. I ain't too proud to tell you that. I'm not ashamed to admit that they have something we don't. They are a freak of nature and I don't need to tell you what could happen if they continue. The people out there in the world have got their eyes closed, but ours, ours are wide open. We have an infestation, a problem to be dealt with. We all know what you do when you get overrun with pests. You eliminate, you exterminate, you eradicate. You send them a clear message that they're not welcome in your home. That is why we are here today. Who are we?"

"Real Worlders!" they replied.

"And what do we fight for?"

"Our world. Our rights. Our life," the group chanted.

"We have Aaron to thank for confirming our information today. He risked his life to bring us this and, not only that, he has made our task easier. One of the freaks, Joanna Westwood, is no longer an issue."

The group's synchronized gasp of awe filled Megan with pride. It was true that the boy had nearly messed up everything by getting caught but he'd risen to the challenge. He'd even eliminated the spy. They had a lot to be thankful for.

For the next couple of hours, Megan talked the group through the plan. To strike the Westwoods now while they were vulnerable, would give them an opportunity too good to pass up. She would not allow witches to take over her world. The world belonged to humans. The world belonged to her.

Chapter Nineteen

"I'm a witch, aren't I?" Aero whispered. She looked up from her uneaten breakfast and stared intensely at her mother. Her thirst for the truth, to solve the mystery, had at last led her here. She had finally put all the pieces of the puzzle together. It seemed so obvious now, she couldn't understand how she hadn't seen it before. Her aunt had been trying to tell her since she had come to stay with them. In fact, she had tried to tell her when they were in the conservatory, until her mother had stepped in and stopped her. Her mother, who had been lying to her for her entire life. Aero needed to understand her mother's choices. Why had she kept this from her?

Her mother had told her she'd been protecting her, but was that true? Aero had always believed she'd been inadequate, she had always felt she didn't have her mother's trust. Now, she wondered if that was just another lie spun to keep her in the dark.

With bowl in hand, Aero saw her aunt swirl her spoon around thoughtfully. She approached the table to sit down but at the last minute thought better of it. She flashed a soft smile at Aero that imparted love and understanding and placed her bowl back on the table.

"I think I'll leave you two to talk," her aunt said, clearing her throat.

Aero noticed her damp eyes before she wandered away. A part of her wanted to beg her not to go. To stay and play peacemaker between her and her mum. *What if she needed her help?*

Aero knew her aunt hadn't meant to cause any trouble and put herself in the middle of things, but since Grandma had been gone, whether she wanted it or not, the baton had unintentionally been passed to her. With the secret out in the open at last, Aero hoped she made her proud.

"How long have you known?" her mum asked softly.

Aero looked out across the garden, and the beautiful blossom hanging on the tree. Life, just like those precious flowers, was hanging in the balance. She rubbed at her hands awkwardly and struggled to meet her mother's gaze, but when she finally did she saw acceptance in her eyes. Her mother looked at her as an equal, and Aero understood that her mother finally saw her as the adult she had become.

"Not long and what feels like forever. I've always felt different..." Aero replied. "Why didn't you tell me?"

"Take my hand, darling. I know you've seen how sad I've been since Grandma left and I know how much you're hurting. I want you to know that I didn't mean to do that, to make it worse, and I never meant to lie to you. Look outside, Aero, you can see the blossom in the garden. It's beautiful, isn't it? The world is full of beauty, wonders and love, Aero, but none of it would ever be enough for me without you. None of it would ever be as beautiful without you here. I thought what I was doing was keeping you safe. There are people out there in the world who are afraid of us, just because we are different. They fear it because of what we are and what we can do. Fear is a dangerous thing, Aero, but I see now that it's me who has made you afraid and for that I'm so very sorry. Sorrier than you could ever know. I may be a witch but I'm only human."

Aero saw her mum shrug her shoulders as if to show her that she wasn't perfect. She then wrapped her arms around her and held her tightly. Aero returned the hug and let out a long breath, as if she had been holding it her entire life. Aero saw no deceit in her mother's eyes and could hear the truth in her words. She forgave her immediately. The two of them had both been dealing with the pain of Grandma Joanna's death and each had locked themselves away from the other. All they could do now was come together and move forward. Louise came back into the room, stepped up to the kitchen table, and put her arms around them both. The three of them sobbed on each other's shoulders, until there were no more tears to cry.

Suddenly, Perri sat up at the table and exclaimed, "Aero honey, I think you are going to be very sick today. I don't think you'll be going to school at all, I'm afraid."

Both Aero and Louise looked up at her, puzzled. "Yes, but you won't really be sick," she reassured them. "I think instead we shall spend the day together and you can learn all about the Westwoods. I'm afraid that some of it is family history, so don't get too excited."

Aero waited for Mum to make the brief phone call to school and, after a large helping of pancakes, the three women sat down together. Her mum got out the old family photo album, as well as a few treasured old books Aero had never seen before. She felt desperate to get to them, especially once she caught a glimpse of a familiar symbol on one of the covers, but she sat and listened as her mother told of her heritage, waiting patiently to get to the best bits. She had to confess that her family history had got a lot more interesting now she had discovered they were witches. She listened as her mother told her about the women, and her mouth fell open in awe and amazement at their power and bravery.

Aero briefly learned that, aside from mastery of the basics of witchcraft, each of the Westwood women had a special power. Joanna had been the most powerful amongst them and had mastery over the Shadow Realm. Perri had the ability of transformation and her favoured animal was the peregrine falcon. It was her transformational ability that had made the tomatoes appear. Her aunt possessed the ability to cultivate and blend magical herbs, which could be put to a variety of uses. Each of the women before her had been gifted with a unique power and no two witches were alike. In time, she too would discover her talents.

Hearing of the women in her family made her look at her dad in a fresh new wave of love. He had known the risks and had still chosen her mother and her family. She always knew he was a wonderful person, but now she loved him even more, if such a thing were possible.

"Grandma was murdered?" Aero had forgiven her mother almost completely for keeping the truth of her witch heritage a secret. At the very least she understood why she had done it, but this new revelation felt like one truth too many. She suddenly felt overcome with a new emotion – guilt.

She had come to understand why her mother had chosen to keep the secret of their family just that, a secret. But in the last few hours she had discovered a secret government unit working with their parents, that her grandma had been working for them, and that there was a group calling themselves the Real Worlders out to destroy them. Simply because they were witches. Of all the things Aero had hoped to learn, this new revelation was the hardest and most shocking to hear.

Aero felt her mum's intense stare, watching her to see how this new information would affect her, but she could also see her determination to strip away all the secrets, no matter how hard they were to accept.

"Being a witch doesn't mean it's all fun and games, Aero. We are what we are, it is our destiny and, with courage, our responsibility too. Your grandma knew the risks she was taking, and she still chose to defend us. She chose to fight for what she believed in. If you had known our secret, it would not have changed her choices. Joanna knew the consequences of her actions, my darling, and she loved us very much."

Aero took the news with a quiet calmness. Now was the time to show her mum she had grown up. She wanted desperately to prove once and for all that she had matured and could handle this. It would take time to process everything she had learnt. Her eagerness to play at being a witch dissolved into the air. The seriousness of the situation landed on her shoulders with a thud. What had been done could not be changed and now her own choices were laid out like a rocky path ahead of her. She wished her grandma was here, there were so many things she wanted to tell her, but for now she needed to resolve herself with everything it meant to be a witch. The powers were not things to be played with like a childhood game and things were so much worse than she could have ever imagined.

"When you're ready, Aero, I think it would be best if Aunt Louise takes you under her wing. She will be your guide but the steps you need to take will come from you. It won't be easy but know that I'm here and that I love you, always."

Aero usually turned to Lilly for advice, and with news this big she was desperate to run to her. To tell her everything. Lilly would know what to do, she was the sensible one, but how could she tell her? Knowing what she knew now, confiding in Lilly would put her in even more danger. Even being friends with her could put her life at risk. She didn't even know why her grandma had been murdered, but if those people, the Real Worlders, were out to kill them all then, surely, they would think nothing of also killing those who were associated with them. *Did this mean she could no longer be friends with Lilly?*

Then there was the matter of the residential, the camping trip. Lilly and she had planned to bunk together. She laughed, thinking back to when they were two innocent friends. *How could they do that now?* The choices in front of Aero were already impossible. She could not bear to lie to her best friend, however well intentioned. Aero herself had been on the receiving end of that, she would not betray Lilly in the same way, she would not break her trust. Whatever she decided to do, it would break her friend's heart. Perhaps, and this would be worse still, whatever she chose, sooner or later, she would lose the only friend she had in this world.

Chapter Twenty

*P*erri watched with anxiety as Aero headed off to get on the school bus the next day. Each of the Westwood women had a role to play, she had been naïve to think her daughter's life would be any different. Still, like any other mother, her stomach knotted with worry and guilt over her decisions. She saw the pain etched in her daughter's face and wanted to be the one who could take it all away. If she could have been the one to suffer instead, she would gladly have taken it.

When they had first moved to Scholarly Wood, she had been so happy that her daughter had made a friend at last. Now fate had cruelly stripped away her happiness. Aero herself had decided to sever the friendship, but Perri knew there had been no choice. Her friendship had been something deeper than that, it had been love. Perri wondered if the old saying, it was better to have loved and lost, than never loved at all, was in any way true. Perhaps it would have been easier for them both if her daughter had never had any friends. Instead it felt like a failure. Or would it be harder to see that love yanked away, only to leave a hole that could never be filled. Joanna had been taken from them, and now Aero would lose Lilly too.

Some bad days came one after the other, like a downpour in the winter time that never seemed to end. The rain was falling so hard now, Perri began to wonder if the sun had forgotten how to shine and the birds could not remember how to fly.

Perri had chosen to make this their home. To stand their ground and not be moved anymore. Something about this place had drawn her to it. The people hunting them were still out there and they wouldn't rest until it was over, until they were dead. As a group, the Westwood family was diminished, their power lessened by the loss of her mother. She only hoped they could give Aero the time she needed to complete her training and stand a chance of defending herself. Wringing out the dish cloth in her hand, her stomach felt like it too understood how it felt to be put through the wringer.

Getting ready that morning Aero had investigated her reflection in the mirror, searching for something different. Besides her unruly hair, she looked nothing like the witches described in the stories she had read. In books, they generally had hideous noses and big pointy black hats. They were old and haggard and covered in warts. Aero thought that her outward reflection did not look anything like those evil witches but inside she felt as if she were exactly the same for what she was about to do to her best friend.

She put off leaving for the bus until the last possible minute, to avoid the possibility of having to hang around at the bus stop with Lilly. Her mum had offered to take her to school in the car, but she knew that would only be delaying the inevitable. There would be countless days after that when she would have to get on the bus and ignore her friend. It wasn't something that would get any easier by delaying it.

Aero looked down the length of the bus as she climbed up the steps. As usual she saw it crammed with children, but she also saw that Lilly had put a bag on the seat next to her to save her a seat.

Lilly, unaware of all that Aero had discovered and its effect, smiled, evidently relieved at her friend's arrival. She had probably begun to think that something was wrong and her friend wasn't coming. Aero could see the thoughts flashing on her friend's face and felt a fresh pang of guilt.

Keeping her eyes to the ground like the coward she was, Aero saw just enough to see that Fred too had an empty seat beside him. She'd always felt a little sorry for him. Aero knew how it felt to have no one like you. She sat down next to him but reminded herself not to be too friendly. From now on she would have to protect herself from the pain of friendship. For the first time in her life she didn't want anyone to like her. When Fred said hi, she muttered a greeting under her breath and got a book out of her rucksack. Pretending to be extremely interested in it, she shut down any conversation, and her heart along with it. She was too afraid to look up and catch her friend's eyes, as she couldn't bear to see the betrayal and hurt in them. Nonetheless, she felt the weight of her friend's stare on the back of her head with all the intensity of a heart breaking, but she couldn't be sure if it was Lilly's or her own.

For as long as Aero could remember she had felt out of control of her life. She supposed it had been the result of the chaos of always moving on and never feeling like she had any foundations on which to cling. Whilst she hated everything about this situation, feeling like she was hurtling down the road in a runaway car, at least this time the hands on the steering wheel were her own. She would do everything she could to become the best witch the Westwood family had ever seen. If there was even the smallest chance she could get rid of these people threatening her family and get back her best friend, she would. That is, if Lilly could ever forgive her.

∞ ∞ ∞

Later that afternoon, Perri opted to run out to the supermarket and get the food in for dinner that night, which meant she wouldn't be there when Aero returned. Louise offered to go instead but in truth Perri hadn't wanted to be home when her daughter arrived back from school. She wasn't sure she could trust herself not to cry.

She took a deep breath. The weight of the last couple of days sagged heavily on Perri's shoulders, but she put on a smile as she brought the bags in from the car. Aero and Louise were engrossed in conversation at the kitchen table, their heads together, Louise laughing at something Aero had said. Perri felt her smile fade and had to confess to feeling a pang of jealousy.

She quickly dismissed the thought and remembered that her sister hadn't been as lucky as her, having never found a special someone. Being close in age, they had always shared everything, and that included Aero. She had no right to be jealous of them now, she just felt she had so much more to lose than her sister. The bond between a mother and daughter was something uniquely special. Nevertheless, she shouted inwardly at herself for her bad behaviour. It felt so good to see Aero cheerful and it was even more wonderful to see the two of them happy.

"I'm home," she said brightly.

"Mum, it's so good to see you. We've been looking at these," Aero replied, bubbling with excitement and pointing at the books. "There's so much to learn but I've already got a knack for it. I can feel it."

"Oh, that's wonderful. Just remember to take it slowly. It's not about knowing all the spells. It's not like a test at school, you don't win prizes for how much stuff you know."

"Oh Perri, she's just excited. There's nothing wrong with a little fun, you know," Louise chipped in.

"Yes, but it's important to take care, Louise, you know that. It's about working together with the magic, you can't wield it like a weapon," she said, defending herself. *Why did it feel like she was always the baddie? Was it such an awful thing for her daughter to have a moment of happiness?* She felt acutely aware that her words had been sharper than she had intended. The anger crept in because of exhaustion and fear. Worry threatened to overwhelm her.

Louise closed the book in front of them. "What about if we have a little bit of a break? Perhaps the three of us can take another look after dinner. I'm sure we'll all feel better after something to eat."

Aero looked up at Perri and said softly, "I'll think I'll go and get on with my homework."

Perri felt ashamed of herself. She walked over to Aero and gave her a hug before she left the room. "I'm sorry, love. I'll get on with dinner now and call you when it's ready. Your dad will be home soon."

"I love you, Mum."

"Love you more."

Chapter Twenty-One

At the dinner table that evening, Perri found herself chewing her food quietly, so she could listen to the conversation Xander and Aero were having. It seemed such a beautiful, ordinary moment hearing the two catching up on their days. She felt like a sponge, soaking up their love. Despite everything that Aero had been through, she had been incredibly resilient, and Perri began to feel the smile coming back to her lips.

It wasn't long before the topic of conversation got around to all things magical and Xander began to tell the story of the first time Perri did magic for him. The delight in his face shone brightly and, despite the embarrassment of Aero hearing how her mother wooed her father with magical plants and spells, it was good for Perri to hear about the beautiful side of magic. Lately, it had seemed to her more of a curse than a gift.

Perri reached out and held Xander's hand. *Perhaps she had forgotten what a beautiful thing it could be. Trust Xander to be the one to remind her.* Remembering the thrill of using magic had given Perri an idea. Louise was right. Her daughter did deserve a bit of fun and she knew exactly how to do it. There were times when a mother's job was no more or less simple than that.

A few moments later and they had all gathered outside to find out what Perri wanted to show them. The sparkle in Xander and Louise's eyes showed that they had caught on to her idea and wholly approved. They exchanged knowing smiles. Perri closed her eyes for a moment, gathering herself. She then put down her head and raised it again with a dramatic flair. The anticipation made all their pulses beat a little faster.

Perri could see the excitement in Aero's eyes and, giving her no time to think, she transformed. In her place now stood a peregrine falcon. Raising her wings, Perri took to the sky. Feeling the current ruffle through her feathers, she let go of obligations, responsibilities and the weight on her shoulders, and soared through the sky in glee. If anyone noticed this peculiar bird in Scholarly Wood that night and thought it odd that one should be in their neighbourhood, they would have been even more surprised to discover it smiling at them.

Xander felt his eyes begin to water, overwhelmed at his wonderful wife. "Damn, woman," he muttered with pride. All he could do was look on in wonder. Even in this form his wife's eyes shone out from the bird looking back at them. He knew Perri had mastered the full range of magical powers but still chose to be at one with nature. Xander looked across at Aero as she laughed, deep and carefree. Her eyes wide, Xander could see the tiny hairs on their arms stand up as electricity surged through the air. He had never once regretted marrying a witch. His extraordinary wife was not only a wonderful woman and an astonishing witch, but a wonderful mother too.

What more could a man want? They watched on as Perri took her family through an impressive array of animals before finally collapsing. It was a powerful display.

"How does she do that, Aunt Louise? That's incredible!" Aero exclaimed in awe.

"Because she is amazing," Louise replied proudly. Xander looked away as Perri smiled gratefully at her sister. He didn't want to come between them as their grievances slipped away. It seemed more than one relationship had been repaired that day.

"It's easy once you know how, Aero. Just be yourself. It's not a trick. All it takes is to be kind. Open yourself to the possibilities that this earth is about more than you can see and feel. The world has many layers, my darling girl, and those on the surface are but the beginning. Being different may be scary but if you open your heart you will learn that we have much to be grateful for. Each of us is unique in our own way." Perri paused to see if her daughter had followed her.

"The Shadow Realm is the source of our power. Many years ago, the mythical creatures, too exquisite and unique for this world, joined together to form the realm.

Having been driven from the land by humans here, they decided to build a world where all would be welcome, where all would be accepted."

"Wow," Aero replied.

Xander knew Aero had understood as she waited patiently for her mother to explain her role in this magical realm. As Perri wiped the sweat from her brow, it was clear she was obviously exhausted. His wife would give no more lessons tonight.

Xander turned to the special women in his life and said, "Well, I think that's enough excitement for one night. How about we go inside for some pudding, something extra-chocolatey? Oh, and we'd better look at the list of things you need for your trip. You're going next week!"

That evening, Perri knocked on her daughter's bedroom door and waited to be allowed in before entering. Aero lifted her head off the pillow and sat up as her mother perched on the bed beside her. "You know, we're no different than any other mother and daughter, really. I've made the same mistakes as your grandma Joanna, even though I swore I'd do it all differently."

Perri saw Aero's eyes go wide at the thought that Grandma Joanna could make any mistakes but was glad that her daughter stayed quiet when she saw she had more to say.

"Just like she did with me, I didn't notice that my daughter had become all grown up. I'm sorry for being over protective, for not trusting you more, Aero. I think I forgot that magic is wonderous as well as hard work. I'm sorry." The two embraced in a deep hug, and Perri whispered into her daughter's ear, "I'm so very proud of you."

Chapter Twenty-Two

The blasted school trip. Aero's stomach did a flip every time she thought about it. Her anxiety levels spiked at the mere thought of the things she might have to do. The team-building events that were meant to be fun but made her feel exposed. Confidence had never been her strongest skill and now she had the extra worry that simply by going she could be putting everyone in danger. *Perhaps she shouldn't go at all? Perhaps she should spend the rest of her life locked away from the world.* She had almost begun to convince herself of the benefits of a life locked inside a bedroom, when the sounds of her parents arguing downstairs rose to a point that she could hear.

Aero couldn't remember ever hearing them argue before. Desperate to get a better position to hear what they were disagreeing over, she went to the bedroom door, opened it and held her breath.

"Xander, if Aero goes on this trip now it's going to be a disaster. She's only just discovered her powers, not to mention the fact that the people who killed Mum are still out there. How could you even think it's safe for her to go now?"

Exasperated by his silence, Perri waited. Her husband maintained his composure, which only fuelled her fear. Everything she said was true. They were in danger and their daughter had embarked on a dangerous journey of discovery. Arguing with her was no more or less dangerous than arguing with anyone you loved, the weight of the world rested on both their shoulders. Perri saw that Xander recognised her fear but still his warm smile reached her heart.

"Because, my darling, if she doesn't go, she will remain a prisoner. Eventually, she will stop living, we all will, and those people out there will have won. We will still be alive, but we will have given into fear and that amounts to the same thing. Doesn't it? If we aren't careful, my darling, all that Aero will learn is to be terrified of humans and what they can do to us. Or worse, terrified of herself. What kind of life is that for any of us?" he replied.

Perri looked at her husband and knew that this was the reason she had married him. Not only did he show his bravery, he earned her respect over and over. Yet whilst she agreed with him, she didn't have to like it. The air between them seemed to shift.

Trying to hide her worry, Perri looked at Xander. "Well then, what are we going to do to make sure this is the best trip she has ever had?"

∞ ∞ ∞

Their voices lowered and the sounds of her parents talking had become muffled. Aero crept further to the top of the stairs and strained to hear, but she could no longer make out the words. It didn't matter, she'd heard enough; her father was right. Resolve flowed through her every pore and she tingled with the feeling of power at her fingertips. She would not be weak anymore. More importantly, the things about the trip that had made her afraid now seemed insignificant. It didn't matter anymore what Andrew Cole and his 'friends' thought of her. It didn't matter that she was clumsy, or not good at most of the things her friends took for granted, like building rafts or climbing. It would take all of her courage, but she would go on this trip and even though she wasn't going to be with Lilly, she would try her hardest to enjoy it. If, for some reason these people came after her, she would fight them and stand her ground as her mother and father had chosen to. Or, she would die trying, like her grandmother before her.

∞ ∞ ∞

Perri had polished every surface of the house with all the elbow grease she could muster, until it shone. She had been through every drawer in the house. Marvelling at the clutter the family had amassed in only two years, she'd ruthlessly disposed of most of it, and had slept very little. In between, she and Xander had worked on a plan to keep Aero under supervision, whilst ensuring she wouldn't know it. It was no wonder she felt exhausted.

The week moved forward with a ferocious pace as if someone had put it on fast forward. Before she knew it, Perri found the day of the residential trip had arrived.

As she closed the zip on Aero's case with finality, she felt as if she were sealing her daughter's fate. "Well, that's the last of it then." She picked up the list again and exchanged a look with her daughter that seemed to say she had forgotten everything they'd already packed, and they would have no choice but to open the case again. "You've got your sun cream, your hat, and your waterproof coat in case it rains?"

Aero nodded. "Stop worrying, Mum. Everything's in there and some extras. I've packed some of the healing herbs from Aunty

Louise in case I get a cut and I have Grandma's box and cards."

A moment of silence passed between the two of them before Perri replied, "And you know what to do in case of..." She pressed her hands to her face as if to block out the rest of the sentence.

"Yes. At the first sign of any trouble, I'll phone you."

In the last few weeks, Perri had seen her daughter master the basics of magic. If there had ever been a more natural born witch than Aero, her mother had never heard of her. The rate at which she absorbed the teachings was astonishing. Her daughter was undoubtedly talented. They had read every magical book Perri owned and a few more that Joanna had left her, from cover to cover, several times over. Perri had already taught her how to summon them in the event she needed them, and Aero had swiftly mastered the basics of spell casting. Still, Perri feared that she was far from ready to deal with a bunch of lunatics intent on murder.

Perri's father John, had succumbed to cancer some years earlier but, like Xander, he had known what he had been getting into when he married Joanna. So too had John's sister, Perri's aunt, Susan. Perri's cousins didn't possess any magical abilities, but the extra bodies on the ground for patrol would prove useful, so she'd called in a few favours. No way in any realm would she let her daughter go off without protection. The trip was a week long, but between them all they would be able to keep watch. Louise had already left earlier that morning, going ahead the old-fashioned way, by car, to cast protection spells on the campsite.

Five minutes later and Aero, her mum and dad were in the car on their way to the school, where she would take a bus to the campsite. To Aero it felt different to be taking the journey in the comfort of a vehicle with decent suspension, and on any other day she might have looked out the window and appreciated the view. The village of Scholary Wood and Pool House was rustic and bursting with daffodils, daisies and bluebells. The many blossom trees lining the roads were already shedding their petals, which blew in the wind and made the sky alive with pink. Yet, her own thoughts distracted her too much to appreciate it.

Having loaded up the luggage on to the bus, Perri hugged Aero tightly to her chest, not wanting to let her go. "Goodbye, my darling. I hope you have an incredible time."

"Are you sure you're both okay with this?" Aero asked. Her mother's wet eyes made her feel more concerned about her parents than herself. A slight hesitation before they answered only caused her to fret even more.

"We're the ones supposed to be asking you that! Go on, have a good time and don't worry, we'll be fine!"

Once they were home, Xander could see the toll this had taken on his wife and he knew full well she wouldn't be able to relax. Even as he saw her slump into the armchair, there was no peace for her as she checked her phone. A message had arrived from Louise to tell her she had put the protection spell in place. He saw Perri close her eyes, trying desperately to rest. Later that evening it would be her shift, but it seemed to Xander that the more she chased sleep, the further away it slipped.

He brought in a cup of tea and placed it down on the coaster. Kneeling in front of her, he knew his role well enough – to be strong and reliable in times of crisis and even now, with his heart heavy in his chest, there was nowhere else he'd rather be.

He'd telephoned work and requested a week's leave. His boss hadn't been particularly happy about the unexpected holiday, especially as Xander had already taken leave for the funeral, but he'd begrudgingly agreed when Xander had explained that his wife had been struggling following the loss of her mother. The excuse wasn't entirely untrue. He didn't think that Perri had stopped and allowed herself to grieve. In truth she hadn't had a chance to, and he worried it wouldn't hit her until they had time to stop. It didn't matter, he would be here for her, whenever she needed him.

Xander took her hand in his, and gently stroked her fingers. She opened her eyes and smiled at him. Even now they sparkled and gave him goose bumps. He loved her. He loved all his girls, even Louise.

Chapter Twenty-Three

Compressed up against the world and the vast, dark void of space, there existed another dimension of boundless wonder. In a hairline crack, a sliver away, unseen to the people of Earth, stood the Shadow Realm.

Instead of a bright sun, an enormous, bewitched moon, which had been gifted by a night unicorn, lit up this homeland. Far from being bleak and dismal, a beam of light took root in the ground and stretched out along the seams of the realm. Holding the bubble of this dimension together and inside this pocket of space, the starlight grew like icicles on the inside of a frozen bubble of water. It was magical to behold and incredibly beautiful.

In the far corner of this impossible, mystic kingdom rested a lake. Its crystal-clear waters flowed down to endless depths and lapped gently at the shimmering silver sands along its edge.

All shapes and sizes of mystical creatures once lost to our world through the sands of time gathered where the lake met the land.

The ever-hungry waters of the lake were nourished by streams that ran like veins throughout the realm. Beneath its surface many water dwelling creatures had made the lake their home and felt safe within its borders. If a visitor ever came to this dazzling land, they may be lucky enough to catch a glimpse of a pack of mermaids skimming the water's surface, or perhaps see a shoal of delicate sprites floating along the shallows.

On the outskirts of the lake, the trees were dense with leaves, which were a peculiar umbrella shape, but in contrast to the green trees of earth, they were silver and sparkled like diamonds. The forest dwellers had made their home within these trees, seeking protection from the erupting storms that were getting ever more frequent. These included the winged horses, the unicorns and their close relatives, the alicorns. Shrouded in the line of glistening ferns, whose tendrils stretched upwards into the sky, stood the centaurs, dwarves, dragons, imps and hobgoblins.

Each of these creatures had their own unique features which they carried with pride. Within the Shadow Realm each had found a home which brought safety, no longer fearful of the humans who had sought to destroy them on earth. However, a new danger had appeared here, and there were those who wondered how much longer they would be safe.

Within the sphere of this jaw dropping, impossible world, the entire group of mysterious inhabitants had assembled, united in purpose. Without exception, every creature who had ever been treated with disdain and shunned on Earth had found a home in this domain. They gathered in their intense sorrow and felt the loss of Joanna, mourning her passing, knowing without her belief sustaining it, it may destroy their world forever. However, each also recognised a new hope with the birth of a new witch. Across the tides and seas of dimensions they had felt the wave of energy in her first magical encounter. Could this Realm be once again resplendent and renewed?

Lake Arcadia was revered amongst all creatures. This was a special and idyllic place, as all who perished would return here one day, to take their place with the spirits inside the waters. Despite the vast shores of the lake, the animals jostled and wriggled to find a space in the crowd. Even the sky felt the weight of the beautiful and beastly creatures.

The shadow creatures had come, led by their formidable leader, Umbria. In their true form, they hung like a dust cloud in the air, waiting for direction from their intimidating master. Not all creatures in the realm were benevolent but harmony had prevailed for thousands of years. On this day they had all come together peacefully, and any past disagreements were forgotten.

Just like the conjured light that illuminated this world, time stretched differently here. The past, the present and the future collided. Like strings on a web, each spun out with multiple possibilities. The animals had felt the vibrations in the web. Tiny hairline cracks had appeared on the outer edge of the realm.

A face familiar to the creatures of the realm appeared. The shadow creatures drew close. Whilst the creatures wished to celebrate the rising of a new true heart to protect their land, they sensed something was coming, and they were waiting.

Megan stared out of the window like a figurehead on the bow of a ship. Internally, nerves were beginning to give her a stomach ache. Outwardly, not a bead of sweat showed on her face, and it remained stoic. The culmination of months of planning was about to pay its due rewards. With Joanna out of the way, the Westwood family were going to have the day from hell. Still, she had her moments of doubt. *Had she taken on too much? Had she planned it correctly?* The opportunity, though, was almost too delicious. If they could capture the newest witch in the family whilst she was away, the rest would tumble like dominoes. She chewed ferociously on the gum in her mouth and shivered with anticipation.

Megan heard footsteps behind her and then a gentle cough to attract her attention. Turning, she smiled and addressed a man in his early forties. Slim built, he had already lost most of his hair. Although his face looked amicable enough, his icy-blue eyes showed the same steely determination as hers. She had been working with the man known to her only as Jason for the last three years. By day he had earned the trust of Maxwell Chambers, having first worked by his side and later, when Mr Chambers had become head of the unit, becoming his security detail. By night, he fed Megan all the information she could want and more. This was how news of this glorious opportunity had first presented itself.

It was he whom she had trusted to secure the first of the targets. Her experience of his loyalty had proved he would carry out her wishes and ensure this victim remained unharmed. The others might not be so lucky. Megan felt grateful to have a man who could be trusted to get things done in her team, the messy things included.

"It's done?" she enquired.

"Of course, and I sent the text message as you suggested."

"Good, that means Perri won't suspect anything until later. Stopping her might prove difficult, but without the protection charm, we can proceed with the plan."

Megan saw his pride as his chest puffed upwards. She knew he would do anything for his fearless, focussed leader. Megan's expression changed, her eyes flickering with fresh delights.

"I'm sure I can rely on you to help with the next phase. We'd better go if we're going to catch up with the girl."

Chapter Twenty-four

At times like this, Aero wondered if she truly had any magical abilities at all. They had been travelling north for almost an hour, and with every passing minute her stomach flipped over more. The bus travelled along the motorway as it made its way upwards into the hills, their destination at least another hour and a half away. Her head ached, and little beads of sweat had broken out all over her skin. *Do witches get travel sickness?* she wondered.

She always sat close to the front of the bus on a long journey, having experienced this rotten sensation before, but today, alone in her seat, she had no companion to ease the horridness. If Mrs Wood had been with them, it might have been different, but she'd unfortunately been unable to come because of some emergency. Instead, Mr Bore their history teacher accompanied them, but even though he sat just in front of her, he was so engrossed in his book, he hadn't even looked up. If she hadn't been so distracted by the imminent dangers and practising her new-found powers, she might have asked her aunt for a herbal remedy before she left, but she couldn't turn back the clock. Aero clutched a sick bag in her hands and hoped she wouldn't need to use it.

A loud clunking sound from the back of the bus came only moments later. The bus lurched as it lost power, its wheels grinding, and then seemed to spring back into life again, only to stutter once more. Thankfully the children wore seatbelts, but all were thrown forward, causing the material to strain against their shoulders and screams to escape from their lips. Bags slid along the floor, catching ankles as they too lurched forward and back. Various objects that weren't secured were flung into the air, as if becoming weightless in space. Aero's stomach went taut with tension and she felt an eerie sense of premonition coming over her.

∞ ∞ ∞

The driver had the good sense to pull across the lanes and head towards the hard shoulder. Fighting the wheel as the power steering gave way, he felt the true weight of the tonnage of the vehicle. With one final clunk, the last of the power left the bus and the driver began a battle to get to safety in time. He became acutely aware of the traffic hurtling past, veering to avoid them. In the back of his mind, he knew that the bus was full, containing passengers who were too young to have their lives cut short. Yet time slowed and ran impossibly fast all at once.

The driver plotted his route as best he could, fearfully aware they were heading straight for the grassy embankment at the side of the hard shoulder looming towards them. He had no time to focus on the things going on around him and if he had time to make course corrections, he wasn't aware of it. In the blink of an eye, it was over. All the flying objects crashed to the ground and silence fell over the passengers as the bus made its impact and came to rest.

∞ ∞ ∞

Aero blinked, slow and sleepily, testing that her eyes still worked. Gradually becoming aware of her surroundings, she realised her body was straining against the seatbelt, and she wasn't touching the back of the seat at all. Disorientated, it felt like she was doing gymnastics, possibly a headstand.

A sharp shooting pain came from her left shoulder but elsewhere her body appeared to be unhurt. At first, she heard nothing, only a deathly silence until gradually murmurings from the other passengers began to filter through, as they too were realising what had happened. Looking behind, the back of the bus seemed to be jutting up in the air. Returning to investigate the front, Aero clearly saw the door crumpled and crushed against the grassy embankment. Their exit was cut off.

She poked at the belt release with her finger, but it wouldn't give. Jabbing at it more forcefully, she winced as she felt it release. Unclipping it, she slid forwards off the chair, and crawled out by the footwell. Now she was standing, but far from feeling safer, her legs began to sway, and she reached for the chair to steady herself. The groans began to get louder around her and she became vaguely aware of more screams erupting.

She took a few deep breaths and her legs felt steadier. From here, she had a good view of the destruction at the front half of the bus, which had absorbed most of the impact. The driver sat slumped over at the wheel, a small trickle of red running down his face. Aero saw that Mr Bore was also hunched forward in his seat. She glanced over at Fred, who sat on the other side of her, a wave of relief washing over her to see him alive. She then let her eyes fall over the other passengers in her eyeline.

She didn't want to ignore their distress but quickly realised that miraculously most were confused, rather than seriously hurt. As for the others further back, she would have to investigate. *Lilly,* her thoughts whispered. Tears threatened to come but Aero swallowed them back. *Calm, keep breathing,* she reminded herself.

As she had already determined, the impact of the crash had cut off the front exit, but Aero saw the path to the rear of the vehicle remained clear. She had to get everyone off the bus safely and find out if those at the back were still alive.

Walking briskly with determination etched on her face, scanning each seat as she went along, she ignored those who cried out and looked for any silent victims. Aero remembered from doing first aid training at school that those who were quiet might be in shock, or worse. Thankfully, all she saw were cuts and bruises and looks of disgust as she walked on past without paying attention to their cries. Aero tried to ignore the increasing incline as she got further to the back.

Spotting the smashed glasses resting in a pile of debris on the floor, she cried out, "Lilly!" There was no way she could stop herself from crying out. *Please let her be okay, please God,* was all she could think, chanting it in her head over and over. Relief swept across her when she saw Lilly alive. She ran over and knelt in front of her, acutely aware of the creak of the vehicle moving with her sudden action. "Lilly, are you okay?" Her friend's eyes were wide with fear.

"Yes, yes, I'm okay."

Aero's relief evaporated as she saw her friend's pale face and shuddering body. She took off her coat and draped it over her as a makeshift blanket. All thoughts of what had gone on between them vanished. Instead, Aero focussed on this one task. "I have to find a way for us to get out, Lilly. The bus isn't safe. Will you be all right?"

Lilly's answer came softly at first, and then she spoke up with more enthusiasm. "Yes. Go on... go."

Aero hesitated for a moment, tears springing from her eyes once more, as she weighed up concern for her friend over the need to get everyone out of the bus and to safety. Her brain tried to process how she would achieve this, given that the back of the bus was stuck up in the air, balancing precariously over the traffic hurtling past. *Who did she think she was, some kind of super hero?*

Aero tried the emergency bar to open the doors at the side of the bus. Working uphill, she felt the strain in her arms but it didn't budge. Putting her good shoulder into it, she clung on with the other arm, even though it throbbed. She felt the door move slightly but didn't dare give it any more in case she fell out. After a few more grunts and pushes, the bar unjammed and the doors sprang open.

Aero thrust herself into the row of the seats at the back of the bus, as if trying to become one with the fabric, clinging on desperately with her arm that protested angrily under the strain.

She gasped at the sight of the cars and the sudden whizzing sound as they rushed past, perilously close. Some swerved to avoid each other, others only narrowly avoided the bus, which jutted out at a 45-degree angle over the lane but did not completely fill it. She pushed herself back against the seat to steady both her nerves and her arms, which were shaking from the pressure. Recovering herself, her heart sank when she saw the gaping distance and drop between the road and the back of the bus. Not to mention the exit being straight into the path of oncoming vehicles. The distance itself was so large it would put a stop to their escape, the risk too great to attempt to jump without causing broken limbs.

Aero's expression changed. Her mind wandered back to her bag and, more importantly, its contents. Finding it would be no easy task, but if she could... Aero didn't dare let herself get carried away. First things first. One step at a time.

Checking once more on Lilly, she reassured her friend she would return. The commotion on the bus had become frantic now, as more of the children made their way out of their seats. Clambering back down the bus, she skipped over feet and weaved her way much more slowly back to her seat. Dropping to her knees, she scanned every inch of the footwell, looking for her bag where it had once been. It was no longer there, having made an expedition of its own during the crash. In the gloom she found it hard to see anything at all, and the shadows from the trickling light through the window played tricks on her, taunting her with false visions as she searched for it. At last, several seats forward and on the other side, she spotted it.

Fred, still strapped into his seat, hadn't moved at all. His eyes were large and glazed over. Aero couldn't be sure if he even understood what was going on around him. "Fred?" He showed no reaction to her voice. Aero moved over to him and shook him gently on his shoulders, trying to get him to answer her. "Fred. Fred, are you okay?"

He shook his head as if to wipe away the disbelief and looked up at her. "Oh yeah... yes,

I think so." His eyes half-closed, his voice sounded dreamy and unsure. Aero could see no sign he'd hit his head. "Are you hurt at all, are you in pain anywhere?"

"No. Really, I'm okay."

Realising she needed a helping hand and that Fred most likely needed a distraction, she said, "I need that bag, and I need your help. Can you help me, Fred? Can you do that?"

"Erm," he replied uncertainly.

"Fred, we need to move, and we need to do it fast. We're in danger. Unclip your belt and pass me my bag."

He managed to do as he was told and retrieved her bag. Aero immediately opened it to check if the contents were still in one piece. Relieved, she became full of purpose.

"Come on then, Fred. We've got work to do."

Fred got up and followed her, but his actions were sluggish, as if he were on autopilot. Aero didn't have time to question the wisdom of her choice of assistant. She shut out all doubts and headed back down the bus.

Andrew Cole loomed large in front of her. *Just great.* The thought of dealing with his kind of trouble was too much. It felt as if someone were throwing every obstacle in her way. It didn't seem long ago that she'd hoped he would notice her freshly-straightened flowing locks, but now she hoped he wouldn't notice her at all, in fact she prayed that he would ignore her. Not because her hair looked an awful fright, which undoubtedly it did, but because the only way to get her friends to safety would be with the use of magic. Letting Andrew Cole in on a secret like that would be unthinkable. He'd already seen too much with her little display in the playground.

To her surprise, his eyes shined brightly as he fixed his attention on her. With a half-smile he said, "You have a plan, I can see it in your eyes. What do you need me to do?"

Realising that he too had forgotten their petty argument and was now focussed on the task ahead, Aero would accept any help offered. "Keep everyone calm. Try and keep them in their seats if you can, Andrew. I need some space to work. Oh, and the driver and Mr Bore, both are hurt badly, they might be unconscious," she replied.

Nodding his understanding, he let Aero and Fred slip past him and turned around.

"Everyone, I need your attention," his said, his voice authoritative and commanding.

Aero couldn't resist sneaking a peek behind her. *Umm*, she mused, before blocking him out. In contrast to Andrew's, her voice sounded cracked and uncertain. "Come on, Fred, let's crack on. Right, I need a minute, okay. Look after Lilly and make sure I'm not disturbed." Fred muttered his assent and crouched down next to Lilly, whose skin had now turned a horrid shade of grey.

Aero turned her attention back to her mission. First, she wanted to steer the traffic away from the bus. If she'd had more time previously to practise, she might have been able to use a cloaking spell, but it didn't help dwelling on what she couldn't do. Instead, she believed she could use a protection charm. This spell was usually used to ward off unwanted magic, but it might also have the effect of creating a bubble of safety around the vehicle. It had to be worth a shot and if she believed, if she pledged herself to the protection of the Shadow Realm, she could do it.

As her aunt and mother had been teaching her over the last week, she prepared the spell.

A pang of sadness came over her as she recalled that her grandma had performed spells just like these. She hoped she would make her proud.

Forces of good, hear my voice, beloved creatures, know my heart is true.

I call on you for your protection, rise up and hear me now.

Friends of Joanna, now my friends too, I pledge myself, my heart, its truth.

A surge of heat passed through her as the magic rushed in like a wave. As it crept over her entire body, she felt cocooned, untouchable, warm and safe. Feeling the power of magic inside her, like electricity, she knew then what her mother had meant. The power felt addictive, she could only liken it to an adrenaline rush. It seemed incredibly easy to see how something like this could become overwhelming. How it might dominate the user, rather than the other way around.

Mindful to remember her desire to do good and follow her family's example, Aero drew an imaginary line that swept out and around the vehicle, placing them inside the protective bubble. Without realising why they were doing it, the drivers of the cars around them immediately began to move over to the outer lane. She'd done it. *Nothing to it,* she laughed, whilst blowing on her fingers, pretending they were guns.

With no time to celebrate her small victory, Aero needed to get the occupants of the bus out to the safety of the hard shoulder. Then she wondered if she really needed to at all. The emergency services would surely arrive soon. A crash like this that interfered with the flow of traffic should have got their attention. *How long did it take them to get to the scene of a crash? Would they send out ambulances? Yes, they would,* she thought, but still she worried it would take too long.

Nodding to herself, she came to a decision. Whilst she'd successfully put up the protective spell, she didn't know how long it would last. All those who could walk would be safer on the bank than inside the bus. The only issue was, how to actually do it.

Reaching for the rucksack, she pulled out one of the jars Aunt Louise had given her. She'd retrieved the bag because of the potions inside and thankfully, even in all its adventures around the bus during the crash, the precious cargo had remained intact. In truth, though, she had been putting off using it because of what it meant. She had already walked out of a friendship because of magic. Doing this would be hard to explain and harder still to walk away from, but she'd made her mind up. She had no choice – the crash had forced her hand. Reaching for the transformation potion, she released the lid, leant out over the back of the bus and sprinkled a few drops onto the road below. There was no need to enchant the potion with a spell as it already contained all the magic she needed, thanks to the talents of her aunt.

Almost immediately, a flash of green emerging from the tarmac caught her eye. *It was working!* As she watched, the enchanted seedling grew, twisting and turning as it cracked through the tarmac. Noises behind her drew her attention away from the fast-growing shoot. Turning, she saw that both Fred and Andrew were looking at her with quizzical expressions on their faces.

"What the heck?" asked Fred, his eyes wide with disbelief.

Aero saw from his expression that, despite his confusion, he appeared to at least be back with them, even if he didn't have a clue what was going on. Whilst trying to think of some way to explain the sudden mysterious vine that had shot up out of nowhere, Aero suddenly noticed that Millie had appeared.

Keeping her back to her, Aero snuck the jar into her rucksack before Millie could catch a glimpse. Turning again to face her, Aero tried to put on a smile that said, I'm not panicking about you catching me doing magic.

"So, what's going on here, then?" Millie asked.

Things had been going so well, but right on cue, trouble had shown up. A minuscule change in the atmosphere made Aero feel suddenly nervous, and she wiped her sweaty palms on her clothes. The memory of working with Millie on the art project floated precariously to the surface of her mind.

"Nothing really. We were just trying to see if there was a way to get everyone off the bus," Aero replied as calmly as she could.

Still, she felt the colour drain from her cheeks. She tried to think of how to handle the situation and could only think about bees for some reason. *Don't bother them and they won't bother you.* Aero looked over at Andrew, looking for clues as to his thoughts. Which side would he choose?

The blank expression on his face proved to Aero that he had no idea how dangerous things had suddenly become. Millie was not a person to mess with. Whenever she was involved, the best thing to do was to make her think she had been the one to come up with all the ideas. It wasn't wise to approach her without a plan.

"Why would you want to get everybody off, Aero? Surely you can't think it's safer out there?"

Aero shifted from one foot to the other, not daring to look outside and alert Millie to her plan. Aero whispered as quietly as she could, "No, of course not. You're right, it's much too dangerous out there."

She was breaking her own rule to be stronger now and stand up for herself more. Sometimes being strong was about playing the long game. At least, that was what she told herself.

Aero nearly jumped out of her skin as Fred gently snuck past her and put himself between them. After a further brief moment, Andrew turned sharply to also take up a position of strength. Earlier she had mistaken his look for indifference or ignorance, now she saw it was a stony wall, one that would not be breached.

Aero took a sidestep, then another. She had no idea how this was going to play out.

Andrew gave a polite smile. "Millie, would you take Fred here and check back on the driver? He's not doing so good."

Aero kept her eyes firmly fixed on the floor, chanting in her head, *don't bother them and they won't bother you.*

Aero saw Millie arch her eyebrows as if deciding if this was something she wanted to do or not. "Well, I guess, as it's you that's doing the asking," she replied with a coy smile. She grabbed hold of Fred's arm and trotted away.

"Erm... you might want to get that, Aero. I presume that's our way out of here?" Andrew said with a prod to her ribs.

Turning back to the plant, Aero saw what he meant, and reached out for the thick vine that she hoped would act like a rope for them to climb down. Andrew, it seemed, had no trouble believing his eyes.

Smiling up at him, Aero replied, "Well, don't just stand there. Give us a hand, then."

He got down onto his bottom, dangled his feet over the lip of the back and helped her to pull it inside. As they drew the rope-like vine into the bus, he looked her in the eyes, shrugged his shoulders, and said, "I guess I've always wanted to believe in magic."

"Shhh, keep your voice down, Andy." Aero glanced back behind her. There was a still an edge of panic that Millie would return, she didn't want to advertise her powers. Still, she sighed with relief that at least she didn't have to hold this secret in with Andrew. As the two caught each other's eyes, they smiled knowingly at one another.

Chapter Twenty-Five

Maxwell Chambers drummed his twitchy fingers on the dashboard in front of him, but his fingers weren't the only thing getting itchy. He'd been sat in the car for around thirty minutes, waiting for the Westwood family to emerge, but already his patience had worn thin. He'd parked a discreet distance away between two thick leafy trees which lined the pavements of Cauldon avenue. It was the perfect spot for him to observe the Westwoods without risking being seen himself.

His brain itched with the thought that perhaps Jason wasn't being entirely honest with him. He started to doubt the information he'd been given. A seed of doubt about his most trusted associate was trying to take root, but he would not justify it. Maxwell could not allow such thoughts to grow in his mind. He owed a lot of his success to him, more than he would be willing to admit out loud.

He shoved it to one side. This wasn't his first stakeout. He'd been 'around the block a few times.' The thing required in these situations was patience. Checking his mobile, he saw no new information had been sent through from headquarters. He held the binoculars to his face and looked inside. *Movement, excellent.*

Jason had provided him with some limited intelligence that Aero had plans to go on a week-long trip without her parents. Unusually for Jason, the information had been somewhat sketchy. Maxwell knew that today would be the day of the trip, but he only had mid-morning as their approximate departure time.

Getting access to the girl inside the family home, whilst not impossible, would be foolish and dangerous. Instead, his plan was to intercept her once the parents were out of the way. Grabbing her for a little one on one chat offered a much more promising proposition than breaking into a protected house of powerful witches, even with Joanna gone. Aero would work with them or they would be forced to take a different approach. He could not allow such dangerous creatures to roam unchecked and unrestrained. He took a deep breath and reminded himself to focus on one thing at a time.

Maxwell zoomed in on the residents inside the home. He could only see Xander, the father, in full view of the window. Whilst an intriguing person for his choice of associations, he was dispensable and not the target. Still, Max guessed from his movements inside that their little trip was about to begin. For the first time that morning, he relaxed a little. *Nice one, Jason.*

Inside the house, still slumped in the chair, Perri's worry twisted tighter and tighter inside her like a corkscrew. She knew that Louise should have returned by now, and the more she thought about it, the more she felt the text message her sister had sent through sounded off somehow. It gnawed away at her until she wasn't sure if her thoughts were just her being paranoid, or if her hunch that something awful had happened was true. Getting to her feet with a renewed sense of purpose, she shouted, "Xander, I can't just sit here waiting. I'm going to go mad. Louise should have been back by now. It feels like a bad omen. Where is she?"

Perri, understandably upset, felt her anxiety levels rising at their inactivity and struggled to catch her breath.

"I don't know but I'm sure there's a reasonable explanation. I don't like this either, and we're not going to get answers sitting here. You're right, we should go."

Perri pulled her husband in for a kiss. She should have known he would support her. The two decided they could wait no longer and made their way to the car. The change from hopelessness to action gave Perri a renewed sense of energy. *At least they were doing something.* They were going to find out exactly what was going on and what had happened to Louise.

∞ ∞ ∞

To his satisfaction, Maxwell saw signs of life and the front door opening to 42 Cauldon avenue. As two worried faces emerged from the house, his smile began to falter. Just a few moments later and Maxwell Chambers found himself cursing. *What? Where was the girl?* It didn't take him long to realise his instincts had been right. He'd been deceived, but he didn't know why.

If Jason had been with him in the car in that moment, he would have shown him exactly how he felt about colleagues who thought they could betray him. There was nothing he could do as he watched the two get in the car and drive away, leaving him empty handed.

∞ ∞ ∞

Aero had heard sirens before. A fleeting sense of panic would wash over her as she wondered briefly who they were for, hoping that whoever they were rushing towards wasn't seriously hurt. This time the sirens sounded almost melodic to her ears. It felt like a victory march as she realised the sirens in the distance were for them. Help was coming.

By this point, all the children, except for Andrew and Aero, were sitting in the relative safety of the grassy bank. Getting Lilly out had been difficult but, with Fred and Andrew's help, they'd managed it together. Still, it felt like a huge relief that help was close by as Aero had a feeling that Lilly would need it sooner rather than later.

Fred opted to stay with Lilly and the other children on the grassy bank. The pupils seemed subdued and quiet but grateful to be alive and out of the bus. A few of them had raised an eyebrow at their means of exit but most seemed too thankful to comment. Aero supposed that like her, they were grateful for the sirens coming to their aid. She imagined they felt as she did inside the bus, as if it were a coffin.

Andrew stayed with her to check on the driver. Despite her discomfort, she didn't want to leave the driver by himself in his fragile condition. Too heavy to move, Andrew and Aero together rolled him onto his side, as close to the recovery position as they could get. In a way he looked almost serene as he lay motionless in the seat, but Aero knew his injuries were serious, otherwise he would have woken up by now. The first aid training hadn't covered this, but it would all be okay now, help had arrived.

Moving to the door to get a better view, Aero shouted and waved her arms. "Over here." Thrilled to see the ambulance pull up next to the bus, she said, "The driver, he needs your help, quickly."

As the two paramedics strode towards the bus, Andrew moved to one side. He assumed that more ambulances would be arriving to help the kids outside, but he selfishly hoped to stay inside the bus a little longer.

He had already decided that he wouldn't leave until Aero felt ready, but unlike her, Andrew felt safe inside. In there, with just the two of them, the layers of his outer shell could slip away. The moment the bus had crashed had rendered them all equal, leaving him free to put the role he had to play behind him too. The part of him that felt like a monster, the part that was his father's son, had disappeared briefly, but once they left, the spell would be broken. His feelings for Aero could never be anything more than a dream. He hadn't lied when he told Aero he had always wanted to believe in magic, because in fairy tales there was always the chance of redemption. With magic there was the hope of a happy ending.

The first paramedic, a woman, stepped onto the bus and strolled first past him and then Aero to reach the front. The woman wasted no time and immediately busied herself with assessing the driver's condition. Andrew saw the relief wash over Aero's face and then a wave of something else flash across it.

"Excuse me?" she asked.

Andrew saw Aero trying to attract the woman's attention. Raising her voice, Aero spoke up louder and then shouted, "Excuse me! My friend is outside. She's badly hurt too."

Aero's pleas went unheard, the woman oblivious to her. Andrew saw the panic rising in her expression, like a dangerous undercurrent was pulling his friend under once again.

As the second paramedic approached, Andrew watched as Aero's desperation to get help to Lilly overwhelmed her. As the man carried the stretcher up the central walkway, he saw hope in her eyes that she would have better luck with him. Instead, the man wedged the hand-held stretcher he carried onto its side between him and Aero, cutting them off from each other.

Thanks to his father, Andrew had more experience at defending himself than others his age, but he was still taken by surprise. He hadn't expected an attack from someone coming to their aid. In a blur of movement, despite attempting to throw a punch, the man got there first, hitting him squarely on the jaw. In panic, Andrew tried to scramble out of the man's clutches.

Aero watched on in horror, helpless to do anything. In the split second of the attack, the woman behind her had grabbed her too. As the dawning realisation came over her that they were both in grave danger, it was already too late. She felt a sharp prick in the back of her arm, and her legs quickly became like jelly. The world turned into a cloudy dream, running in blurry slow motion. She saw a fleeting glimpse of Andrew through half-closed eyes as the man lunged towards him, pinning him with an assault. She felt the weight of her heart beating inside her chest and had a moment's hope as Andrew tried to break free and rescue her. His eyes wide with fear, he continued to struggle, but it was hopeless. The man loomed over him and used his weight to throw him to the floor, leaving him crumpled as if he were nothing more than an old piece of paper.

Aero watched on silently, her heart filling with dread as she saw Andrew motionless and floppy on the floor. She tried to sit up, but her body wouldn't obey her commands. Grasping for her will to overcome whatever the substance in her body was doing, she realised it was a battle she could not win. The darkness of unconsciousness struck her as her world went black.

∞ ∞ ∞

Megan and Jason chatted quietly between themselves as they carried Aero to the fake ambulance. Jason made sure the children could not identify their cargo by using his body to block their view. A bunch of teenagers might be irritating, troublesome even, under different circumstances, but they were hardly a threat in their current state. Still, it worked to the pair's advantage if they would assume the person on the stretcher belonged to the injured driver. By the time the children realized something was wrong, they would be long gone. Aside of course from the roles they were playing, it would be highly doubtful that any would remember their physical appearance.

With Aero secured and out of it, Jason hopped into the driver's seat, switched on the sirens and headed off. Megan allowed herself a smile and a fresh piece of gum.

Chapter Twenty-Six

Louise craned her neck up to identify the source of the light. Whilst she couldn't hear the irritating hum, the flickering of the electric tube was more than annoying enough. It didn't distract her from the awful situation she found herself in, though. As she sat and contemplated her fate in the gloomy room, knowing that was probably what the kidnappers wanted her to do, her spirits dropped, rather like an early morning fog sweeping in unexpectedly. She mused that her own guilt, the most futile of all the emotions in her opinion, rather than the people, was the hardest thing to fight. She'd let her niece down and she'd let her sister down, just as she had her mother. Whilst she wished desperately that she could do something about the situation, her hope began to fade. Louise was not only trapped in the cold, dank room but also inside her own feelings of frustration. The kidnappers had succeeded at robbing her of almost every drop of hope.

She had no idea if she was still alone in the building. She couldn't hear anything but with her blasted ears, that didn't mean much. Her magic was useless. It would be easy to succumb and give in to the desperation. She looked around her. Even if she'd wanted to do something, her arms were strapped to an old tattered chair which had seen better days, the plastic cords snaring her arms in a lion's grip. The floor had a thick coating of dust and dirt. Layers of old smells accumulated in her nostrils, making her choke. In the corner of the room an old radiator clanged faintly but the room was empty of anything useful. Time had no place in here, and Louise had no idea of how many minutes or hours had passed, but her mother hadn't brought her up to be a quitter. She was a Westwood, a name that stood for resilience and never giving up. Still, she couldn't help but feel helplessness threaten, and tears budded in her eyes. This room could easily be the last place she might ever see but she couldn't let her anxiety put her off. If she gave in now, she would destroy herself inch by inch, saving the kidnappers the job.

She quickly dismissed her first idea of rocking the chair to one side, in favour of one that wouldn't leave her with a broken arm or leg. Whilst her arms were bound to the chair, her legs were free. Which meant she at least had the use of those. A younger, sprightlier person could manoeuvre themselves to their feet significantly more easily than her, possibly even elegantly. She, however, could no longer class herself as young, despite the advantage of being magical. She decided it didn't matter how it looked, or how she struggled with the exertion. If there was a way to get to her feet, no matter how ugly, it could be the start of an escape – it was not the how that mattered.

She moved her feet to give her a position that matched as close to a straddle as possible and then strained to lift herself. Locking her knees as best she could from her sitting position, she ignored the burning through her thighs. She stumbled back to the ground on her first attempt, jolting her with a flash of pain. She ignored it and tried again, and on the fourth attempt found herself standing with a chair strapped to her back. *Finally*, she thought, out of breath from the effort. The question was what to do next. Shuffling across the floor with her burden, she hoped that the chair would give up as she smashed it against the wall. If anyone was out there beyond the locked door they would hear, but Louise had no other option. Heaving as she spun, she committed completely to her act of vandalism. With hindsight, Louise thought that she should have tested out her own strength before whacking the chair quite so hard. It disintegrated far more easily than she'd imagined, causing her to jar against the wall and land heavily. She knew that later an angry looking bruise would appear on her arm, if she survived to see it. She felt the sting of splintered wood and warm liquid ran down her arm.

There was no time to dwell on it. Overhead, the electric light began to burn fiercely. It burned white hot, until with a gigantic crack, one that even she heard, the electric light surged and went out. *What's going on?* she wondered.

∞ ∞ ∞

"Hello, this is Max Chambers." Tiresome as phoning in to Control was, Max had no other choice. He needed some direction on what to do next, now that the smallest of the Westwoods had eluded him, thanks to a little backstabbing. Whilst he was the head of the unit, he still had bosses to answer to.

"Passcode?" the robotic voice on the other end asked.

"Achilles." Max couldn't help but think that the bloody operator should have been able to recognise his voice by now. He squeezed the hand not holding the phone into a tight fist. The whole charade with passcodes and passwords reminded him of foolish children's games. The only game he had in mind was one of revenge on Jason, but it would have to wait.

"Connecting you now, Mr Chambers."

The phone clicked as the operator connected him.

"Requesting directive, base. Negative acquisition of target. Request next steps." Max squeezed out each word carefully, suppressing the seething rage he felt. He knew full well he would have to give a report and take an ear bashing for his failure upon his return, but he realised that anger wouldn't help him now.

"Report back to base immediately. We have detected a huge surge in dimensional energy. Your immediate return is requested."

Max understood that *requested* meant if he didn't come back, then he might as well not bother, but it wasn't as if he had any better ideas. He couldn't comprehend what would cause such a surge. His knowledge of other realms and universes was somewhat limited. He was aware that the unit monitored such things, but he had difficulty comprehending any world beyond his own. He supposed in a way that was why this job mattered to him in the first place. The Westwoods were something he could monitor and account for, even if his eyes grew wide with disbelief at the things they could do.

The possibilities of other worlds existing beyond his own, well, that would take a little more getting used to. The proof that witches existed was quite enough. Max shuddered just thinking about it. Whilst he would never admit it openly, his needs were that of a simple man. From now on, a solitary one with only two needs: a position of power, and loyalty. He would bite his tongue, play errand boy, do whatever was necessary to hang on to his power. As for the other - well, Max thought, you win some, you lose some. "I'm on my way now."

"Try to make it quick." The short reply was anything but polite.

Chapter Twenty-Seven

Aero's eyes blinked one after the other as if they couldn't agree with each other about the timing. When they finally opened in unison, the world around appeared hazy and unfocused, but she could feel the rumble of the road beneath her. Despite the lazy workings of her brain she determined they were still travelling in the fake ambulance. She tried and failed to move her arms, then realised her body had been strapped to a trolley. The man and woman responsible for kidnapping her and hurting Andrew, or maybe worse (but she wouldn't let her mind go there), were both seated up front.

She didn't want to dwell on all the things she should have said to Andrew back at the bus, if he didn't make it either. He'd been the last person she thought she could rely on and he'd surprised her. Aero stopped herself. That line of thinking wouldn't get her anywhere. She wouldn't start saying goodbye to him just yet. She wouldn't give up.

Perhaps they didn't expect her to wake up yet? That would make sense because, whilst she couldn't make out what they were saying, they did nothing to mask the sounds of their voices. *There was plenty about magic she didn't know, maybe the way drugs worked on her was another part of the deal? Perhaps her metabolism worked faster?* Whether it turned out to be another ability or not, Aero knew she was not immortal and she knew she had to stay alive. Not just for herself but for Lilly and for Andrew.

Aero strained to decipher what the kidnappers were saying, trying to find out any small detail of their plan. Whilst the voices were unintelligible over the sounds of the vehicle, she could hear what sounded like laughter. The sinister chuckles punctuated the silence of the journey with an unnerving tone, making her feel even more afraid.

The crunch of gravel beneath the wheels and the jolt of the van coming to a stop put a halt to any more thinking time. Wherever their intended destination, they had arrived. Aero understood that playing dead, or rather pretending to still be asleep, could be the only thing to keep her alive. Closing her eyes felt like they were lifting weights. Her body screamed at her to keep them open, but she took a deep breath and willed herself to go still. The doors to the ambulance creaked open and she felt a thud as the pair lifted her out and began to wheel her. To where, she had no idea. Feeling may have returned to her limbs, but as her mind cleared from the drug, her body filled with dread.

Aero believed they had taken her inside a building of some sort but didn't dare open her eyes to confirm it. They were greeted by several other voices, who addressed their questions and delight to the woman. They appeared to be discussing their plan without a thought for her, as she lay like a forgotten slab of meat next to them. From the sounds of the conversation it seemed the woman who had kidnapped her was the one in charge of this radical group. The man who had assisted her asked permission to leave. After a brief exchange, the voices dissipated, and Aero realised they had left her there alone.

The desire to do something, to act on the opportunity, became a throb throughout her entire body. Postponing it until the last possible moment, at last she dared to look.

Louise blinked quickly, trying to speed up the process of getting used to the dark. If this was the kidnapper's crazy way of scaring her, then she wanted to be prepared. She had a pretty good idea who they were, the people who had taken her. There was only one group they could belong to: 'The Real Worlders'. The ones who had killed her mother. The stain of it was still fresh in her mind.

"Hello, Louise."

Her eyes had now adjusted sufficiently to the darkness to be able to make out the shape before her. She immediately wished they hadn't. Gasping, Louise staggered backwards. Standing before her was someone who resembled her mother in every detail, even down to what she had been wearing last.

"Whatever kind of joke this is, I can assure you it's not funny. Surely even kidnappers draw a line at impersonating a dead person?" Louise snapped, her patience worn thin.

"Please, don't be afraid. Forgive me for startling you." The entity, (this was the only word that sprang to mind to describe the thing in front of her) immediately became a cloud of dust, and then puffed out like an explosion. It imploded, becoming solid once again, until standing before her was a man.

"I am Umbria, from the Shadow Realm. I have come to rescue you and your kin."

As she looked at Umbria suspiciously, Louise found herself drawn to the dark pools of its eyes, which seemed to go on forever. She looked away for fear of losing herself inside them. Aside from the obvious evidence of Umbria's shape-shifting abilities, something about the creature's manifestation unnerved her. The Shadow Realm, the source of their power, had always been a place within her, rather than something that could physically exist. *Was it possible he was telling the truth?*

Pointing behind him, Louise could now see a hole, or rather what looked like a bubble in the wall. A link between this world and the silvery domain that lay beyond.

"It will take courage to cross through, but understand I am not a patient being and I do not go around making a habit of rescuing people," Umbria said.

Louise looked at him, still undecided if this might still be all a part of some elaborate trick. "If you think that appearing as my mother will somehow make me cooperate with you then you are very much mistaken. Joanna is dead, how dare you pretend to be her!"

"I touched your mother before I came through, which explains my appearance as I arrived in your world. I am sorry for any distress I caused but know that I will not apologise again. I am a being unloved by your world and I do not wish to be in here longer than necessary. My presence here is not something I do because I want to."

"But how could you touch her? I don't understand."

"You are a Westwood, are you not?"

Louise nodded. Looking up at his face fearfully, she deliberately avoided his eyes. Instinctively, she tried to jump back again as Umbria reached out to her, but her body had already reached the furthest barrier her makeshift cell would allow.

"All things are possible in the Shadow Realm. Be brave."

Taking a deep breath, she held out her hand and allowed the creature to touch the bare skin of her hand. She witnessed the emergence of her mirror image, otherwise she would not have believed it. Now, she looked more closely at the manifestation and saw herself. Louise suddenly understood what it was about Umbria that had unnerved her so. He was not of this world and merely projected himself upon it. Every form Umbria took would be a mask of his true self, no matter how precisely replicated it appeared to be.

Umbria smiled at her knowingly. "Shall we go?" he asked, already aware that his shape changing had convinced her to trust him.

"Well, there's the small matter of my kin to rescue before we can leave. I don't know if my niece is being held here too but I'm guessing they have kidnapped her. I'm sure the only reason they took me, a useless old witch, was to keep me out of the way. Why else would I have been left in this draughty, smelly place without even a cup of tea? Whether or not you care to be here, if what you say is true and you're here to help, then I will not leave until I've found her."

Umbria had no idea what a cup of tea was, but he understood the message clearly enough.

Chapter Twenty-Eight

*P*erri tried to phone Louise several times as Xander drove the same route Aero and her classmates had taken earlier that day. With no answer from her sister, the feeling of trepidation increased with every passing mile. Whilst their progress was always going to be faster in a car, Xander took full advantage of the use of the motorway and paid no attention to the speed limits. That was, until they came to a skidding halt behind a huge line of queueing traffic.

"This isn't right, Xander," Perri said with panic etched on her face. Then in a hushed voice that was nothing more than a whisper, she added, "Aero." Trepidation turned to terror in Perri's stomach and as she looked at her husband, he nodded. Conversation was unnecessary, both of them understood what the other needed. Switching off the engine, Xander pulled out a blanket from the back seat and held it around his wife. If anyone had been looking they might have assumed a change of clothes was taking place, which might have given rise to curiosity but not concern. Instead, Perri was about to do what Xander could not: give them a bird's-eye view.

Xander rolled down the window. Perri didn't hold back and took to the air immediately. Whilst they would normally, not that there was anything normal about this situation, be praying no one would pay any attention to the bizarre sight of a bird flying out of a car window, neither really cared. The only thing on their minds was their daughter.

All Xander could do was wait as Perri flew off in search of the cause of the traffic.

All Perri could do was implore the Realm to keep her daughter safe and hope her premonition would prove to be wrong.

It wasn't long before Perri found the reason for the queuing traffic. First she spotted the fire engines, ambulances and police cars. This was quickly followed by the sight of the tow truck attempting to move the bus and unclog the lanes, confirming her worst fears. As she searched desperately for her daughter in the chaos, she realised the impossibility of trying to make out individual faces from this high vantage point. There was nothing else for it, she would have to go down there. The only question which remained was whether to stay in bird form or transform back. She thought it over for less than a second. If she were to get the answers needed, she knew she would have to change back. Throwing every aspect of caution to the wind, she found a hidden spot behind a tree.

Appearing as if out of thin air, Perri looked around and wondered where to start. On the grassy embankment sat only a few children. *Where has everyone else gone?* She presumed they had been taken to hospital, which only exacerbated her fear and make it harder to decide what to do next. At the front of the bus stood a large, bright yellow recovery vehicle and a man busy attaching the tow bar. *Was it called a boom?* She couldn't remember.

Then she spotted a fire crew but realised she'd seen no fire. Whatever had caused the accident remained a mystery to her and perhaps to them as well. Perri quickly concluded that they were probably at the scene to manage the situation rather than deal with any blazing infernos.

Hearing sounds of moving cars, she noticed the cones behind her and saw that they had successfully re-opened one of the lanes. The people in the vehicles moved slowly, mostly because they were intent on looking as they drove past, but they were moving again.

Answers were needed. *Was Aero alive or dead?* She would have to risk speaking to someone, she needed to know. She headed straight towards one of the fire crew, who appeared to be directing the others. She determined by his stance that he was the one most likely in charge. As she approached, his eyes grew wide with confusion.

"Er, miss. Who are you? Where did you come from?" he asked, looking around as if to confirm his questions and the utter strangeness of a person appearing out of nowhere.

The look of puzzlement on the man's face was not lost on her but she decided to push on. "Yes, I'm one of the school support staff. I was following behind in my car." Perri waved her arm in the general direction of the traffic and hoped her lie would suffice.

"Ah, I see. Well, how can I help?" His tone softened as her explanation did its job. "As you can see, we're extremely busy sorting all of this out. There's still a few children to evacuate."

"Yes, I just wondered if you could tell me where they've gone – the children?" Then, Perri subtly added, almost as an afterthought, "Was anyone hurt, or killed?"

Once more, he eyed her suspiciously. Perri supposed he might be trying to determine if she were a nosy person who had decided to interfere in their work, or if she were who she claimed to be. Seemingly satisfied, he replied, "All of the children, except those still waiting on the bank, were taken to the local hospital. Hang on, I'll get Jed to give you the details.

"Jed?" he shouted across to a portly gentleman, who looked up and replied, "I'll be right with you."

Before turning back to his work, the man said, "I'm so sorry to tell you the driver passed away en route to the hospital. He's a hero, really. I think it's likely his quick thinking saved the rest of the passengers. Most of the students were suffering with light injuries and shock. There were several in a critical condition but so far, I haven't heard of any other fatalities. You'll need to check with the hospital though. The school has been informed and they're setting up a help line now for parents to find out more information. That's all I can really tell you for now. If you don't mind I have to get back to it. I'll let Jed give you the information you need."

Thanking the man, Perri sighed deeply in relief, then quickly chastised herself. A man had died, but her Aero, her darling girl, would be all right. A few minutes later and Perri had all the details she needed from Jed. As nice as he was, it didn't take Perri long before she seized her opportunity to slip away, leaving him somewhat bewildered.

Reunited with Xander in the car, the traffic now moved freely. Perri informed Xander of their destination, and his face paled as he listened. Gripping the steering wheel tightly, he fixed his eyes straight ahead as they passed the site of the crash. Taking the next turning off, they prayed their daughter would still be alive when they made it to the hospital.

∞ ∞ ∞

Arriving back at headquarters, Maxwell's stomach reeled as he saw the look of anger on Arianna's face. To put it mildly, she did not look at all happy.

"Glad you could finally join us," she said, lifting her eyebrows in contempt.

Somewhat in shock at the sight of Arianna herself, the statement implied something more than frustration on her behalf at his tardiness. Without a clue how to respond, not knowing what he had done wrong or why his boss would be so angry with him, he chose to remain silent.

"Nothing to say about the cock-up this morning?" she enquired.

"I understand you must be upset," Maxwell replied. Gathering himself, he opened his mouth to put her straight, but didn't get the chance. Interrupting him, she looked flabbergasted.

"Upset? That doesn't even begin to cover it."

"May I explain? That's not unreasonable, is it?" Maxwell asked.

"Would you like me to tell you what's unreasonable, Maxwell? Because, like it or not, I'm going to. I put you in charge of this group because I believed in you. Yes, they told me you were young and inexperienced, but what I thought I saw in you was drive, passion and ambition. Now all I see is failure and your disasters reflect on me. Bad-ly." She weighted each syllable to emphasise her point. "Jason gave you all the information you needed to secure the girl. I don't know whether you just couldn't be bothered or if you screwed it up but frankly, I don't care either way. I don't have the time or inclination to listen to your excuses."

"But I didn't screw it up, Arianna. I was fed the wrong information."

"It's Miss Campbell to you, and yes, you screwed up. You made a monumental error and you are no longer in charge of this unit. I am only here until Jason returns, and when he does, you will report to him. Jason phoned me earlier to inform me that you hadn't secured the girl, and he was in pursuit. Those bloody people have got her, thanks to your mess. Those terrorists have got themselves a witch. Oh, and we have a dimensional spike as well, so that's another thing I need to sort out. All I know right now is that looking at your face is giving me a headache. Get out of my sight and try not to screw anything else up."

If Maxwell had been angry before, his mood had boiled to a level that could only be reached from the stratosphere. Perhaps Arianna had been right about his inexperience, but she'd been wrong about this being his screw up. He cursed himself for allowing his feelings of friendship to blind him to this betrayal. He would have to suck it up though, because there wasn't a damn thing he could do about it.

Chapter Twenty-Nine

*L*eft in the corridor like a patient in an overcrowded hospital, Aero lay on the bed she found herself strapped to. She could see no way to escape, and no rescuer coming to her aid. Her bag and its contents were nowhere to be seen, and with it the herbs, her phone and any hope. She felt utterly alone. For the first time since her kidnapping, she had a chance to reflect on the hopelessness of her situation. She was going to die here, or worse, they were going to use her powers against her will. The training she'd done hadn't covered that. *Could she prevent them from using her?*

∞ ∞ ∞

Louise looked on as Umbria once more dissolved in front of her and became a cloud of dust. She felt the bindings from her hand go loose as Umbria released her. Rubbing at her wrists to restore the feeling, there was no time to reflect on what was going to happen next. Instead, she watched as the dust melded into the metal lock of the door, which then swung open. Frozen for a moment, scared stiff of stepping out of the room that had held her prisoner and into the unknown, Louise didn't know what to do. The indecision lasted only seconds; the shame of her capture would not continue, she would not let her family down again.

Her poor hearing being of no use in this situation, Louise peeked around the door, first in one direction and then the other. *Empty.* Umbria's presence made her uncomfortable but right now he gave her the only hope she had of saving Aero. She followed his trail of dust down the empty, shadowy corridors, which made Louise feel like she was a rat in a maze. Allowing Umbria to lead the way, Louise proceeded slowly. It wasn't cowardice that compelled her to be cautious. Louise knew that if she were to rescue her niece, getting caught again was not an option. Besides, Louise decided that Umbria seemed more than capable of getting out of any situation, without any help from her.

They aimlessly tracked through the corridors, looking for any clue as to the whereabouts of her niece, who could be anywhere. Louise had no proof that Aero was even in this building and yet she felt her energy. She remembered reading that when one sense is impaired, the others take over. She supposed the people stating this didn't consider magic as a sense. As she allowed Umbria to go behind the doors she could not, her pace increased. Her confidence grew. *She could feel Aero. Her niece was alive!*

Suddenly, Louise saw something ahead. Slinking back as small as possible into the wall for fear of being seen, she held her breath. Nothing wrong with her sense of smell, Louise had to stop herself gagging from the odour of her own sweat hitting her nose. Fear made her skin prickle as she realised it was Aero, lying on a bed, up ahead. From this distance she couldn't determine what had happened to her niece, but the pull of magic felt so intense, she knew that Aero had somehow managed to stay alive.

She sensed someone was leaning over her niece, stroking her hair. Louise's eyes narrowed as she felt a surge of rage pulse through her body. Aero appeared to have been left in the corridor. Goosebumps rose up on her arms, and she shuddered from holding in the anger. *How dare they do this to her!*

The person began to speak but the softness of the voice made it indecipherable. The beat of Louise's heart throbbed with a pulse that echoed her desire to intervene. To swat this boy away from her girl, like an irritating fly. Yet, Louise considered her actions carefully. *Where were the others?*

As the man stroked her hair, his fingers tickled her skin. Aero shuddered, inwardly shaking with every touch. Terrified she would be sick, she tried to focus her mind on something good, something far away from this moment, but all she could think about was Lilly and Andrew. The time for this charade had almost ended, as she knew they couldn't possibly believe she was still under sedation. Aero knew nothing of the drugs they had administered to force sleep upon her, and had lost all sense of time, but she understood this game had to end.

She listened to the soft tone of the man's voice as he spoke to her. Seemingly unaware of her small movements, he had yet to realise his prisoner had awoken. As he continued to talk, she began to realise the man at her side was only young, perhaps not that much older than herself, and that he was giving her a confession. This person had killed her grandma and decided to tell her about it. The murderer stood close enough for her to smell the breath on his lips and feel it on her skin.

She listened to every word as he told her of the evening of Joanna's death. It was clear that he felt remorse for her accidental death but something else more terrifying lingered beneath his words. He felt justified in the killing. As he spoke to her of the Real Worlders, he talked of them as if they had taken justice to new heights. They, her family, were a blight to be eliminated from the world. Each word was said with such vile hatred, yet his voice remained calm, and all the while he continued to stroke her hair.

Aero had never been the kind of girl to feel violent. She was many things; shy, awkward, lacking in confidence, but as her head began to throb listening to the sounds of this boy's voice, her anger twisted inward. *Who were they to think themselves so much better?* Her fists coiled into a tight ball, as the only thing on her mind became bitter revenge. She would show them justice.

Whack. At the sound of the noise, Aero's eyes shot open and the top half of her body sprang up, trying to break free of the bed. In the space where Jason had been only a moment before stood a fearful gigantic thing, and Jason lay crumpled on the floor at his feet. Terrified of this new horror, Aero pulled hard at the straps holding her wrists to the bed, but they wouldn't give. The creature's bony body sent chills through her body, its appearance too terrifying to be anything other than a nightmare. She wondered for an instant if she were hallucinating.

Despite her fear, Aero found herself longing for the creature to bring an end to the boy. He had killed her grandma, and only moments ago she had been ready to dole out her own swift justice. Instead, out of the gloom behind him, a familiar face appeared.

"Auntie?" Aero whispered.

The unnameable creature disappeared before her eyes and in its place hovered a glittering collection of silver dust. Of all the bizarre dreams she'd had recently, this had to be the strangest.

"Sshh." Louise put her fingers to her lips.

Aero did her best to help her aunt make short work of the straps holding her down. Aero followed her request to be quiet and took the help of her aunt's steadying arm underneath to help her off the bed. Wobbling unsteadily at first, she soon caught herself and stood unaided. Taking hold of Louise's hand, Aero began to tug her towards the exit. Louise shook her head, no, vehemently, and tugged at her sleeve, pulling her in the other direction.

As they started heading back into the building, Aero glared at her aunt in desperation. Not daring to draw attention to themselves by raising her voice, she had no choice but to follow. As they slid inside the room which had held Louise prisoner, Umbria, having taken on human form once again, closed and locked the door behind them.

"Aero, you're alive!" Louise threw her arms around her niece and held her tightly. "Where are the guards?"

Backing away from Umbria suspiciously, Aero replied, "I don't know! They all disappeared, saying something about dimensions spiking. I've no idea what they were on about."

"And what about the boy? Do you know who he is?"

Aero hesitated. The thought of telling her scared her a little. She had no idea how her aunt would take the news. *Would she react as she had done and go after him?*

"He's the one who killed Grandma, but it was an accident. He didn't mean to do it." Keeping it brief, she realised that omitting the pride she'd heard in the boy's voice would be for both their benefit.

"Well, there's no time to dwell on it now. Aero, meet Umbria."

Still somewhat afraid of a shape-shifting creature, Aero stayed silent.

"He's from the Shadow Realm. Look behind you, that's where we're going."

"Auntie, what are you talking about?" Her body trembled as she turned and saw what could only be described as a bubble and a hole meddled together in the wall. *How did she miss tha*

A booming sound coming from the other side of the door signalled their captors had discovered them, and they were coming in.

"There's no time. Come on!"

Aero didn't dare to think of it as an escape and fully expected to hit her head on the wall as they sprinted through the bubble together. A part of her had now become certain she was under the effects of some powerful hallucinogenic but as she followed her aunt through the bubble, she caught a glimpse of silver and gasped as she found she had been transported to another world.

Chapter Thirty

As Aero stepped out of the bubble, with Aunt Louise and Umbria at her side, her steps felt like the first ones taken by astronauts on the moon. Each footfall landed on crunching, silver dust, leaving an original footprint in this new and alien domain. Looking into her aunt's face, Aero could tell from her astonished expression that she too felt overcome. They had simply taken one step and entered an exquisite new world. For the second time in her short life, everything about her reality would be different from now on. She could never again look upon her own world with the same two eyes.

A wave of panic crashed over Aero and she swung around. Only seconds ago, she had expected to feel the weight of a hand capturing her from behind, but she needn't have worried. The bubble which formed the bridge between their worlds had sealed behind them.

She seemed to be stumbling from one panic attack to the next. Taking a few steadying breaths, Aero didn't let her thoughts linger on the possibility that they were now trapped inside the Shadow Realm. If she held this level of anxiety for much longer, Aero felt certain her heart or lungs or legs or body would simply give up and cry game over. Her heart pounded so heavily in her chest it made her ribs ache. It simply had to stop. Aero ground to a halt and slid to the floor.

Willing the words to come out calmly, Aero said, "Auntie, wait! I need to catch my breath, and I need to ask you something. Am I going mad?"

Kneeling, Louise gently cupped her niece's face in her hands. "My love, if you're going mad, then so am I, but I can assure you that we're doing it together."

Running her hands over the ground beneath her, Aero confirmed with tactile touch that which her brain could not understand. They were really, physically there.

"We'd best not dawdle. Come along, the creatures are waiting, and we have someone to meet. Besides, my debt is repaid, and I wish to return to my own kind," Umbria urged.

Taken aback by his words, Louise enquired, "Debt? What are you talking about, Umbria?"

"Simply that a favour was owed, and I have returned it. Or I will have, once we reach the meeting place. So, please do come on."

Somewhat recovered, Aero got to her feet and the trio began to walk. Intrigue and curiosity drove the Westwood women on as they walked beneath the unfamiliar speckled sky. The shimmering stars and moon overhead were just the beginning of the strangeness of this new land. The Shadow Realm was a place of wonder and uniqueness. Louise and Aero followed Umbria as they tracked along the sandy shores of Lake Arcadia. Their heads turned towards the sounds of chittering, to see rainbow-coloured sprites delicately hovering over the water.

"We are definitely not in Kansas anymore," Louise laughed.

Aero found it hard to take anything in as she looked around in dazed wonder at the myriad of creatures. It was as if some person had collected together a list of mythical creatures and put them here in a magical wonderland or zoo. Aero turned to Louise in disbelief. "I'm okay, just can't quite believe it's real, that's all," Aero said, shaking herself.

As they walked onwards, they headed in the direction of a cottage on the outskirts of a densely packed forest. The sound of twigs snapping made the pair jump and scream out loud and Louise thought she saw shadowy movements coming from within the trees. She found herself taking a sharp breath as a unicorn stepped out from beneath the branches. It didn't approach but simply watched them.

Reaching the door to the cottage, which looked as if the trees from the adjacent forest had simply been hacked from the ground and then stacked on top of each other to make the walls, Umbria said, "Now you must knock."

"But why? Who's in there?" Aero demanded, feeling overwhelmingly homesick and terrified all at once.

"A friend. There is no need for fear."

The small cottage was hardly imposing to look at, but Aero couldn't help thinking of the story of Hansel and Gretel. From what she had seen so far, she would be right to expect anything behind the front door. Thoughts of evil witches sprang to mind. Glancing from the door to her aunt, she said, "I can't do this, Auntie."

"That's okay. I'll do it love, but stand back, just in case." As if feeling the weight of unseen eyes upon her, Louise edged forward gingerly and rapped on the door.

Aero took a step back and waited, the throb of adrenaline coursing through her veins. As she shuffled from one foot to the other, her feet quickly froze and her heart skipped a beat as, with a creak, the door opened.

"Mum?" Louise asked, eyeing up the person in front of her with a mixture of suspicion, curiosity and heartbreak.

Aero saw the disbelief flash across her face and knew her aunt was thinking the same as her, it simply couldn't be Joanna. Aero felt certain her jaw hitting the floor must have made a huge thudding sound, but she didn't hear a peep.

"Thank the realm you're here, and thank you too, Umbria," Joanna said.

"You are welcome. I hope I have cleared my debt. And now, if you don't mind, I wish to return to my family."

"Of course. May the starlight be with you," Joanna replied, bowing deeply in respect.

"Grandma!" Aero cried. All thoughts of caution thrown to the wind, she flung her arms around her. Sighing deeply, she pulled her grandma into a tight hug. As she inhaled she immediately recognised the sweet-smelling perfume.

"Well, I can confirm that this is Grandma," Aero said matter-of-factly.

"I'm glad we've confirmed that, Aero!" she replied with a chuckle.

Having thought she would never hear it again, Aero couldn't help but think how good it felt to hear her laugh.

"Now, come on in. We've got a lot to talk about but first I must ask that you do not tell me anything of the outside world, of Earth. I do not know when we are meeting each other. It does not do a witch good to know what is in her future. Or is it the past? Honestly, I'm not sure."

"I guess I'm all ears," Louise replied, as they followed Joanna into the cottage. Inside, moss covered the walls of the modest space. To the right, Aero saw a table and a collection of utensils in a makeshift kitchen. In the left-hand corner stood a small wooden bed, and in the centre were several chairs. Louise took the first seat she saw and put her head down between her knees to stave off the nausea.

"Aero, go and get your aunt some water from that bucket over there."

Louise underwent several bouts of stomach-clenching moments but eventually recovered enough to sit upright again. It wasn't every day that she came face to face with her dead mother.

"I'm so glad to see you are both okay. When Umbria came to tell me you were in danger, I don't mind telling you my heart skipped more than a beat or two."

"Grandma, I don't understand how you can be here," Aero exclaimed.

Her grandma moved in swiftly, placing her arm on her shoulder and said, "Stop. Whatever you are thinking, you must stop. Here in the realm, time is suspended. The past, the present and the future all squish together rather like a cake. If you are from my future you might tell me something that will affect us being here. So it's best not to, my dear."

"Okay, I think I sort of understand. You're saying it's timey wimey? Just like in Doctor

Who?" Aero asked with a glimmer of understanding. She quickly concluded that if her grandma told her pigs really did fly in the realm, she would have believed her. From now on she would believe everything she heard, maybe even crop circles.

This version of her grandma could only be in her recent past. For one thing, she had recognised Aero immediately. Not telling her that back on Earth she had died felt wrong in every way possible, but she bit down hard on her tongue and listened.

"Well, sort of. Except, of course, this is all entirely real," Grandma Joanna said with a wink. "I must have been about four or five when I first discovered that I could visit here. Back then I thought it was all a dream. I could visit the Shadow Realm through the bubble and go back to Earth as if no time had passed at all. For a child, a place like this is, well, it's a place of marvels and wild adventures!"

Aero sucked in a breath and felt her eyes well up. "But you never told us, you never told me about it? Why not?"

"I don't really know, Aero, except to say it always felt like it was my secret to keep.

Somewhere deep inside, I just knew that. I am so glad to see you here now, though."

By the time the three had finished talking, Aero and Louise had come to understand that Joanna frequented the Shadow Realm often. So regularly, in fact, that the inhabitants had helped her to build this cottage. On one such visit, Umbria had come to tell her their kind had sensed danger to her family. It appeared the shadow creatures were somehow connected to the Earth and more specifically to them. Aero never did learn what favour Umbria had repaid her grandma, but she felt grateful to have had him rescue them nonetheless.

Joanna told them of the cracks in the fabric of the realm. How she feared that something dreadful might be coming. Aero didn't dare to say it out loud, but she suspected that the cracks were somehow related to her grandma's death. *If the Shadow Realm were to die, what would happen to the creatures and to their powers?* She pushed the thought to one side, having already been an unwitting hero enough for one day. She felt fully justified in feeling her duty had been fulfilled. After all, what could a girl like her do about the collapse of another dimension, having only just discovered it?

∞　∞　∞

When the time came for Louise and Aero to return home, neither wanted to leave.

"Can we not just stay here with you, Grandma?" Aero asked.

"Oh, my girl, I wish you could. I too must leave soon, but how about this. Before you go, I'll introduce you to someone. His name is Constello."

Out of the forest, from where he had been watching, the night unicorn, Constello, appeared. Aero felt the hairs on the back of her neck stand up on end. His coat jet black, Aero could not take her eyes off his mane and tail, which she swore were full of stars.

"It's my great pleasure to meet you both," Constello said, his deep bow giving both Louise and Aero a glimpse of his magnificent horn. "May I ask to when it is you would wish to return?"

Grandma Joanna added, "Constello is the keeper of the gateways between our worlds."

"I suppose it goes without saying that we can't go back and stop the bus crash?" Aero enquired, feeling she already knew the answer.

Joanna nodded.

"Well then, can we go to the hospital? I have to find out if Lilly and Andrew are okay."

Constello bent down his front legs until his horn touched the earth. His mane shimmered as it flowed with the movement. A sizzling metallic tang hung in the air and Aero gasped at the sight of a bubble, through which she could see the hospital.

"May the starlight be with you, Louise and Aero," Constello said.

"Before you go, Aero, I think you should know that now you have been here, if the realm is in danger, you will hear its call." Joanna looked around her as if assessing the damage. "I fear that may be sooner than either of us would like."

"But what could I do to help, Grandma? And what about the Real Worlders? When we get back, won't they still be after us?"

"There will always be those who wish to destroy us, Aero, but for now I think you should be safe. I'm sure they will be scurrying around wondering where you two have disappeared to! As for the realm, we, that is, all the Westwoods, have an obligation to protect it, whether we wish to or not."

A little crease appeared on Aero's forehead. She would leave with an ache in her heart, knowing that on the other side, a world existed where her grandma did not. She held her head high and, together with her aunt, stepped through the bubble.

Chapter Thirty-One

"We are gathered here today to celebrate the life of Andrew Cole. A life struck down in its prime. A flower cut from the earth before it had a chance to blossom. Yet we do not measure the quality of a life based on the number of its pages. Instead we must look to its content."

Aero let the words of the priest drift away. She could hardly believe that she had to face the pain of another death. Gathering together so soon at the parish church in Lake Rode felt painful, exposing the hurt of her grandma's death all over again. But this time there had been no question in her mind about attending the funeral. She'd had no difficulty making the decision to go.

She supposed she had been walking a tightrope the last few years of her life, afraid to step forward for fear of falling, but now she had been compelled to move. Her steps were just as dangerous, perhaps more so now she had been made aware of the danger lurking beneath her. Still, there was no choice but to keep moving forward.

She trembled slightly. It always seemed to be cold inside the church, whatever the time of year. Wrapping her grandma's scarf around her, she inhaled deeply but could no longer smell any trace of her perfume. Still, she imagined that she could. Finding comfort in the softness of the material, she held onto the ends with her hands. It gave her something to do. Something precious to focus on.

She looked across the church at Andrew's father. Sat in the front row of pews, behind the coffin, his face reminded her of the stone statues that adorned the church gravesite - stony and hard. Yet, she could see that his eyes betrayed the sadness beneath his icy exterior and his face glistened with fresh tears. Like him, she wished she'd had more time. Time to get to know the real Andrew, the one she had met on the bus when the genuine Andrew had been exposed, revealing the kind-hearted person beneath the mask. She had only just begun to know him and there were so many things about his life that were still a mystery to her.

If he had a mother, she wasn't here today. Which made her think that perhaps it had been just Andrew and his dad. Aero let go of the scarf and reached for her mum. Gently squeezing her hand, she also let go of the ball of emotion inside her stomach, releasing the ache that had been in her chest since she'd learned of Andrew's death. With it, the tears she had been unable to cry came falling to her cheeks.

She was glad to see a lot of pupils from Pool House attending. Andrew had always been popular amongst his tribe, but it felt comforting to see so many other faces, many of whom had been on the bus with her. Lilly and Fred were sitting with her. Aero had kept her promise to be truthful to her best friend, telling her everything that had occurred that day, including the real reason Andrew had died. The two had decided that Fred too should know the truth and now they were a band of three. Stronger together, united in grief.

Aero took out a tissue from her pocket and dabbed gently at her eyes. She hoped the mascara she wore wouldn't run down her face. She scanned the church for something to focus her attention on, only to catch another glimpse of the shiny mahogany box that carried her dead friend. The sparkle of the lights reflecting on its surface reminded her of the light going out in his eyes.

The last time she had seen Andrew he'd been left to die on the dirty floor of the bus. He'd rushed to her aid, only to face the ultimate price. Which now left her with two impossible thoughts: she never thought someone would die because of her and she'd never realised she would come to think of him as a friend. The images of his motionless body were committed to her memory, this portrait would forever hang in the deep crevices of her mind. Lilly, Fred and her family knew the truth of his death but to everyone else, Andrew had been an unlucky victim of a bus crash.

It would remain just another secret for the Westwood family to keep. It sometimes felt as if they were so wrapped up in secrets it had become impossible to remember what lay underneath.

At the time of discovering his death at the hospital, Aero's mum and dad had not entirely understood the significance. Clearly their thoughts had been for Aero. She could only imagine how scary it must have been for them when they discovered Aero was missing. Still, since learning of how an ordinary boy from school had died trying to save her, they had seen what Grandma Joanna wanted them to know. There were people who would seek to eradicate them for reasons no logical person could understand, but there were also those willing to fight, and lay down their life for them.

Mum had told her that, like Grandma's death, it would be better for the truth to remain hidden. Those people who were a part of the government had ensured it would stay buried, leaving Aero somewhat conflicted.

Andrew had shown his courage and humanity the day of the crash. He had been a hero, but no one would ever know. All she could hope for now was that wherever he'd ended up, (she believed in heaven now as well as crop circles), he would find his happy ending at least.

Before she knew it, the end of the service arrived. As Aero contemplated whether going to the wake would be something she could cope with, her dad turned to her and said, "I think we could all do with something disgustingly gooey and chocolatey. Fred, Lilly, are you going to come back to our house too?"

Trust her dad to know exactly the right thing to do. Lilly slipped her hand inside Aero's and Fred took Lilly's, as they began to walk out of the church together. Aero couldn't help but notice how Fred's gaze lingered upon her friend and how Lilly smiled as she caught his stare.

Epilogue

The year of Aero's seventeenth birthday had certainly been a memorable one. *Was it possible to live a lifetime in only a year?* For her, it felt that way. It had been a year when she had discovered the unbearable depths of loss and found something larger than herself. A journey of discovery. She had come to understand that not everyone in life was who they claimed to be, and it wasn't just her trying to fit in. Everyone, it seemed, wore a mask or held a secret, but not all were easy to see. Not to mention her own secrets. Yet, when some were removed, the person beneath them turned out to not always be the monster they had appeared.

She was a witch! Aero had whispered the words to herself many times since learning the truth, as if saying them aloud could make her feel they were more real. She had felt pain and fear more deeply than she believed any person could but now she knew that her heart had that kind of volume, she felt determined to fill it with something good.

In the cottage, her grandmother had told her that she would hear the call of the Shadow Realm. Whilst she had no idea what she'd meant, she already knew that when she heard it, she would answer, albeit reluctantly. She wouldn't have to do it alone, though. Lilly and Fred knew her secret now. Magic, it seemed, was too large for her to understand by herself, but perhaps love would be the way to make sense of it all. She had a purpose and together they would fulfil it.

Her relationship with her mum was so much better now she didn't see her as just a child. It helped that there was no longer that awkward secret driving a wedge between them. Aero understood she had a lot to learn about being a grown-up; being a witch wasn't the only secret to discover. She still needed to know who she was, navigating life one step a time, like everyone else. But with her mum and her aunt's guidance, she would get through this.

Still, all of that would have to wait for another day. Aero held her grandmother's playing cards in her hands. For now, she had a birthday party to attend. Today she was the star attraction, the magician and the entertainment. They were big shoes to fill. She only hoped she would make her grandma proud.

Jason ordered the unit under his command to continue their investigations into the Shadow Realm. The Westwoods were a threat to civilisation and a liability. Now he was in charge, things were going to run differently. They had not yet come to fully understand the forces involved in the dimensional spikes and subsequent transport, but witnesses had seen it for themselves when the Westwoods escaped their cell. They were making progress, though, and soon they would be able to recreate it for themselves. Despite the memory of their previous failures, Jason smiled. He knew how happy their progress would make Megan.

Silence fell as Umbria rose forth to address the creatures of the realm. "We have gathered here today by the sacred lakes of Arcadia, to discuss our plans. Joanna is dead and a new witch has risen, but it is clear that they have lost their powers. Look around you, my friends, our very existence is crumbling around us as we speak. The realm is cracking apart. I say we should not stand idly by any longer. It is time for us to rise again and reclaim Earth as our own once more."

"What about your debt to Joanna? We have lived in harmony for years, Umbria. You have yet to give this new witch a chance."

"I have repaid my debt. I owe nothing, and I shall not place my fate into the hands of a child."

"And what does Francis have to say about all this. I notice he isn't here. He is, after all, your most trusted advisor."

"Now is the time for those with ambitions larger than our world, Constello. Those that fall behind will get left behind. No exceptions will be made, not even for Francis."

"You're wrong, Umbria. It is in the humblest and smallest of egos that change can ignite and become a fire. Did Joanna teach you nothing?"

"Constello, just like this world, you are a relic, a myth, known only to those foolish enough to believe in fairy tales. With or without you, the shadow creatures are going to return to our homeland. From the dusts of Earth we were born, and it is there we shall return and rule victorious. You, my pointy friend, can do nothing to stop us."

"Your thinking is flawed, Umbria, but as you say, for now I can do nothing. But be warned. If you continue to travel this path, it will mean war."

"In that case, I shall look forward to seeing you on the battle field."

THE END

Other Titles by Sarah Northwood

Also, available on Amazon from Author Sarah Northwood.
Chilling thrillers (18+) that should not be read alone!
The Unravelling: viewBook.at/learnMorenow

The Volunteer: getBook.at/Horror

She's Not Gone
getBook.at/ShesNotGone

Poetry:
Little Moments of Calm
viewbook.at/Littlemoments
Butterfly Dreams
getBook.at/ButterflyDreams
The Truths We Tell
getBook.at/TheTruthsWeTell

Children's Titles:
Legend of the Night Unicorn:
getBook.at/NightUnicorn
Unicorns are real and other cool poems
getBook.at/Unicornsarereal

You can also follow me on facebook for my latest updates.

https://www.facebook.com/SarahNorthwoodAuthor/

Printed in Great Britain
by Amazon